Tiziano let go of her elbow and stepped back so he could lean against the wall and study her.

And the more he looked at her, the more he was certain he'd found the answer to all of his problems.

"What do you dream about, Annie Meeks?" he asked.

"And what will you do with my dreams if I share them with you?" she asked in a tone he could only call challenging. "Assuming I can remember any of them, that is. Fickle things, dreams. It's mostly those who can afford to indulge them who ponce about worrying over them in the first place. The rest of us have work to do."

"What if I made it so you could afford to ponce about at will?" he countered. "Or anything else you like, for that matter."

"And maybe tomorrow morning I'll wake up to find myself the Queen of England," she replied briskly. "But either way, that won't get these files sorted or my rent paid. So if you will please excuse me—"

"Annie," he said, liking the name more and more each time he said it, "I want you to be my mistress."

The Outrageous Accardi Brothers

A marriage deal with two happily-ever-afters...

The two brothers running the notorious Accardi Corporation are total opposites but have the same goal: elevate the Accardi empire.

Known for his playboy antics, wild card Tiziano Accardi has one final chance to prove to his elder brother, Ago, that he's more than his extracurricular activities through a very convenient marriage. But when he makes the most unexpected of choices, both brothers' worlds will be flipped upside down!

Tiziano must marry the innocent Cameron heiress or lose his position in the Accardi Corporation, but he has other plans. And when he bumps into Annie, she becomes the perfect solution to all of his problems...

Read Tiziano and Annie's story in
The Christmas He Claimed the Secretary
Available now!

After a lifetime of clearing up his brother's messes, apologizing to Victoria Cameron is the least Ago can do. Only, he never expected that *they* would share one night or that it would have forever consequences!

Read Ago and Victoria's story in
The Accidental Accardi Heir
Coming soon!

Caitlin Crews

—

THE CHRISTMAS
HE CLAIMED THE
SECRETARY

HARLEQUIN
PRESENTS

ISBN-13: 978-1-335-73890-5

The Christmas He Claimed the Secretary

Copyright © 2022 by Caitlin Crews

Harlequin Enterprises ULC
22 Adelaide St. West, 41st Floor
Toronto, Ontario M5H 4E3, Canada
www.Harlequin.com

Printed in U.S.A.

USA TODAY bestselling, RITA® Award–nominated and critically acclaimed author **Caitlin Crews** has written more than one hundred books and counting. She has a master's and PhD in English literature, thinks everyone should read more category romance and is always available to discuss her beloved alpha heroes. Just ask. She lives in the Pacific Northwest with her comic book artist husband, is always planning her next trip and will never, ever, read all the books in her to-be-read pile. Thank goodness.

Books by Caitlin Crews

Harlequin Presents

The Sicilian's Forgotten Wife
The Bride He Stole for Christmas
Willed to Wed Him

Pregnant Princesses

The Scandal That Made Her His Queen

The Lost Princess Scandal

Crowning His Lost Princess
Reclaiming His Ruined Princess

Visit the Author Profile page
at Harlequin.com for more titles.

CHAPTER ONE

IT WAS NOT the first time in Tiziano Accardi's admittedly splendid life that a woman had fallen at his feet.

The notable difference on this occasion was that the woman in question had not been gazing upon him as she tumbled, tossed to the ground at the very sight of his much-remarked-upon male beauty.

How delightfully novel.

Tiziano, never in much of a hurry at the best of times, was particularly unhurried today. His humorless and deeply boring brother—who was, unfortunately, the stalwart and responsible CEO of Accardi Industries, the keeper of the family purse strings, and, worst of all, distressingly immune to his younger brother's much-vaunted charm no matter how Tiziano tried to win him round—had demanded that Tiziano present himself for his biweekly dressing-down. It would have been a daily occurrence, if Ago had his way, but Tiziano could not always be asked to make an appearance in the office. Not when there were far more interesting places to be. A beach in Rio or the

Philippines, for example. Any of the world's glamorous cities, from Milan to Tokyo and back. Or, really, any other place where beautiful women gathered.

He was something of a connoisseur.

But here in the dreary office he was today, against his better judgment. And will. He had woken up in London for the first time in some weeks this dreary fall, and thanks to the perfidy of his household staff, working in concert with his brother's fearsome executive assistant, Ago knew it.

The thunderous summons had been delivered at top volume, down the phone Tiziano would never have answered had it come from his brother's line.

It was not that Tiziano disliked his role as the company's chief marketing executive—his official title, for his sins. On the contrary, he not only enjoyed the job, he was also—to everyone's great surprise, apparently, given how often it was mentioned in tones of nearly insulting wonder—quite good at it.

A reality that he knew drove his brother rather round the bend.

Because it would be easier to dismiss Tiziano if the younger Accardi brother was nothing more than the empty-headed man-whore the tabloids made him out to be.

It was also true he gave said tabloids ammunition, but he was only a man, after all, and therefore tragically imperfect. He was always the first to say so. Was it his fault that so many beautiful women found him irresistible? Or that because he enjoyed a lively evening out, it was assumed that he was as vapid and fatuous as a great many of the people who tended to take part in those evenings?

The real scandal, Tiziano knew, was that he had actually participated in his brother's bid to make the family company—the one their grandfather had started in Italy and their father had expanded into foreign markets—into the multinational corporation it was today. Complete with its own shiny, glossy headquarters in giddy London, far away from the ancient family heap outside Firenze, awash in wisteria and regret.

Not that such inconvenient facts got in his brother's way when he wanted to deliver a stinging lecture or five. When Ago took it upon himself to roar on, stern and uncompromising and with much talk of *family legacies* and *what is owed to the Accardi name*, neither God nor man could stop him.

Tiziano, who considered himself a bit of both, if he was honest, was well used to the storm and drama of it all.

He even found it all a bit entertaining, usually. Ago *did* like to go on and on and Tiziano quite liked lounging about, acting as if he was as useless as most believed he was. It was a game they played. It reminded him of when they were heedless children, chasing each other across the rolling hills of Tuscany and dodging cypress trees as they ran. How could he not enjoy the adult version of that?

Especially because his brother clearly did not,

growing ever more grim and disapproving in response to Tiziano's indolence. Tiziano had imagined that at some point in the not-so-distant future, he would *actually* find himself sprawled out on the floor of Ago's office, pretending to nap whilst his brother delivered his favorite lecture about *optics*.

In truth, he'd been looking forward to it.

Sadly this fall, the lectures had turned to distressing orders to take up the old ball and chain, a dismal enterprise that Tiziano had intended to happily avoid for the rest of his life. After all, he was the spare to the Accardi fortune, thank you. Not the heir. What did it matter how he entertained himself? Empires hung from his brother's stern, uncompromising fingers, not his.

A point Ago did not seem to think mitigated what he believed to be Tiziano's responsibilities.

So it was possible that the sight of the woman before him—who'd been scowling down at the heap of file folders in her arms as she charged down the stairs that he'd been climbing in as desultory a fashion as possible—was far more intriguing to him than she might normally have been. Particularly when she went down on the landing as they both reached it, falling over what appeared to be her own serviceable pump, then hitting the ground. In an explosion of documents that rained down all around her, she came to a stop a scant centimeter from his big toe.

Clad in hand-tooled leather by the finest artisans in Rome, *naturalmente*.

"I'm well aware of the effect I have on women," Tiziano assured her when she came to a complete stop, and the last of the documents finished its snowy descent to lie on the landing beside her. "But I must give you points for effort, *cara*. Making it rain with a shower of corporate documentation is a lovely touch. Truly."

And on any other day, at any other time, he might have left it at that. He might have nimbly stepped over yet another woman prostrate at his feet and carried on taking the longest route possible to his brother's vast executive suite at the penthouse level of this gleaming tower in the City. On any other day, he would have forgotten her before he made it to the next landing.

But then, this was not any other day.

Because Ago had declared that not only was Tiziano to marry, a horror in and of itself. But more, he was expected to marry the tediously virtuous bride of Ago's choosing. Tiziano knew of the girl in question. Had even met her on several tiresome occasions drenched in respectability and its dire twin, responsibility. She was a nun-like virgin, according to all accounts as well as his own observation, who happened to also be the beloved daughter of one of Accardi Industries' best clients.

Though perhaps *beloved* was not the right word. What was indisputable was that Victoria Cameron was her loathsome father's only daughter. As far as Tiziano could see, the man's fervent desire to control his daughter's matrimonial choices, while making certain they benefited him, was nothing short of medieval. Tiziano would be very much surprised if poor, boring Victoria had ever known the touch of a man. Or had ever spent more than three seconds in the presence of one without her father looking on and jealously guarding over her.

As if an untried convent-bred girl was such a lure in these depraved times that men needed to be restrained in her presence or they might go mad with lust and longing.

It was laughable.

When Tiziano had suggested to his brother that prissy, pearl-clutching moralist Everard Cameron dispense with the theatrics and simply mount a virginity auction the way he clearly wished to do—though without calling it what it was—Ago had only glared at him in that way he did, all steel and disappointment.

That hadn't changed the facts.

Ago intended that Tiziano should be the highest and best bidder for a prize Tiziano did not esteem in the least. What was required of Tiziano was very simple in this case, according to his brother in all his consequence and condescension, handing down dictates from on high. Tiziano need only restrain himself from the worst of his excesses and then, once married and settled and domesticated entirely, confine said excesses to the sacrament of marriage.

Given that Accardis did not divorce, because why divide up properties and assets when it was easy enough to live separate lives on said far-flung estates, his brother was delivering nothing less than a life sentence.

Tiziano liked his life as it was. He was in no particular rush to usher himself into his own cell.

That was why he was still standing there, looking down at the heap of hapless female and corporate documentation at his feet. And that was why he was there to receive the full force of the woman's scowl when she lifted up her head, shoved back a bit of the red hair that had fallen into her eyes, and made it clear that her scowl was no mistake.

By deepening it as she beheld him.

"I can't say it's surprising to discover that a man dressed like you is a waste of space," she said, incredibly. She pushed herself up and looked around, as if taking in what had become of her file folders for the first time. "How chivalrous. By all means, please keep doing whatever it is you were doing. I'm sure it's more important than helping a woman as she *falls down the stairs.*"

Unused to that tone of voice when delivered by a female instead of his brother's deep growl, it took Tiziano a moment to realize that she was *scolding* him.

And then, as if the scowling wasn't enough, the woman simply…ignored him. She set about collecting all her papers, crawling about on the floor before him on her hands and knees. He might have assumed that was another bid for his attention. After all, it did give him quite a view. He had never seen the woman before, but it was clear at a glance that she was one of the innumerable faceless minions who worked here. Probably a secretary, he would wager, or something of that ilk. The pumps she had tripped over were cheap, with scuffed heels, and the undersides were worn away. The pencil skirt she wore was a shade of muddy brown that he doubted anyone would consider fashionable. And as she scuttled about on her hands and knees before him, the cream-colored blouse she had tucked into her skirt pulled up, showing him an intriguing glimpse of shocking pink lace.

He was no callow youth and still, there was something about her that captivated him. Perhaps the way her hips moved this way and that, forcing him to contemplate the span of her waist, and how it might feel to measure her curves with his hands.

It was tempting to assume she was crawling before him for precisely this purpose. To tempt him in just this manner.

But perhaps what really intrigued him was how unselfconscious she seemed. And, more surprising by far, as if she truly could not give a toss whether he stood watching her gather up her papers or not.

It was not a sensation he had ever felt before.

He was Tiziano Accardi. He was not ignored. He could not recall a single moment in his life when he had not received as much attention as possible from everyone and anyone in his vicinity.

And he could not say that he was filled with *ex-*

citement, precisely, that it was occurring now. What he discovered—as one lowering moment followed another while she continued to crawl around the landing, muttering to herself as she stacked up her documents and shoved them back into the folders they'd come from, as if she'd entirely forgotten that she wasn't alone—was that a lifelong question had finally been answered. Here, on an ignominious stairwell landing, on a gray and unremarkable Tuesday in the midst of a gloomy autumn.

He liked to say, and often did say, that it was not *his* fault that he was so magnetic that no one who encountered him could help but make him their focal point in all things. How could they resist? Yet now he discovered that he really did prefer the comfort of forever knowing himself to be the center of everyone's thoughts.

All thanks to this nameless woman who, if he was not mistaken, had actually *dismissed* him.

He told himself that it was in the spirit of discovery, nothing more—certainly not a childish wish to refocus attention where it clearly belonged—that he squatted down before her, relieved her of the file folder she held, then scooped up a huge pile of the remaining papers and tossed them inside.

"That's not actually helpful," she told him. Not quite the sweet thanks he'd expected. She pushed back from all fours so that she was kneeling before him and fixed him with a baleful glare. Another expression he had never before seen on a female face when it was pointed in his direction. Much less from her current position. "You do realize that I have to put them in order, don't you?" But then she let out a laugh. "Who am I kidding? I doubt very much you have the slightest idea what people do with the documents that keep your company chugging along, do you?"

"So you do know who I am." Tiziano smiled. "That is a comfort. For a terrifying moment there I could have sworn that I had become unremarkable."

"And who, may I ask, could possibly avoid knowing you even if they wished it?" Her accent was filled with hints of the north, meaning that where she came from in this cold country was even more frigid and inhospitable than London in the dark of a late, wet autumn—though her cheeks were rosy. He found himself contemplating them with interest. "I was under the impression you dedicated yourself to becoming as ubiquitous as possible before the age of sixteen."

"I'm delighted you noticed," Tiziano drawled, wrenching his attention away from her *cheeks*. "But, *cara*, surely you know that as delightful as all this flirtation is to me, it is in no way wise. You must not need your job overmuch if you are willing to risk it for the chance to sharpen your claws on a man of my stature."

As he watched, more fascinated than he cared to process at the minute, her eyes—a surprising shade of gray that put him in mind of the foggy, moody mornings that were the parts of London he loved best—looked very nearly murderous. She flushed slightly, making her cheeks all the rosier. And while in most women he would assume that was an involuntary, biological response to a perfect specimen such as himself, he rather thought that when it came to this creature, it was all temper.

How extraordinary.

And then she didn't give in to it, which was even more impressive.

Instead, she produced a tight smile. "I must have hit my head when I fell," she said, though Tiziano thought they both knew quite well she had done no such thing. "My apologies. As a matter of fact, I do quite need this job. Thank you for reminding me."

"It is forgotten," Tiziano said with a magnanimous wave of his hand. "But tell me, *cara*, what is it you do here?" He looked down at the file folder in his hand. "A bit of filing, is it?"

"A bit of filing and a bit of typing," she replied, and not in the tones of a woman who revered either of those tasks. But then, neither would he. "They don't call it the secretarial pool these days. But effectively, that's what it is."

"You're a secretary?"

"I am indeed." She cleared her throat, perhaps hearing herself echo back from the walls of the stairwell, because when she looked around again she seemed significantly more flustered than she had before. "My supervisor will not be pleased that it's taking me so long to come back with these files. And that they'll have to be put back in order."

"How long have you worked here?"

She took her time looking back at him, and though she was still attempting that tight smile, her gray gaze had gone suspicious. "A year," she said. "Well. Nearly."

"A year." He tilted his head slightly to one side. "How odd. And yet I'm certain I have never seen you before."

Then, to his amusement, he watched any number of sharp replies rise and fall in that gray gaze of hers. He had to assume each was more acid than the last.

He was oddly disappointed when she did not gift him with any of them. Instead, she smiled wider, though he was certain, somehow, that it did not come easy to her. "Every moment has been a joy."

Tiziano laughed. "I rather doubt that. Whether they call it a secretarial pool or not, it sounds unpleasant. I can't imagine I would enjoy it myself."

But she was not drawn in, another first. "I apologize for my potentially concussed outburst before, sir," she said, and it was all sweet enough. Trouble was, he didn't believe her.

She made as if to rise but he beat her to it, getting to his feet and then reaching down to take her by the elbow and pull her up.

And there was nothing to it, the way he gripped her arm and drew her from the floor. She could have been a grandmother. A child. But he was entirely too aware that she was neither of those things. She was a woman.

More important, she was nothing at all like the exceedingly dull Victoria Cameron.

As far as Tiziano could tell, Victoria had been raised to be, at best, a particular kind of adornment. Her father came from a long line of overbred aristocrats, with various titles knocking about his closet. His daughter had been engineered since birth to appeal to the only sort of man Everard Cameron truly esteemed—that being a man like himself.

His daughter was thus innocent and untouched to suit the dynastic aspirations of a man who needed heirs. And more, wished to go about the making of them with confidence that the sons and daughters who bore his name could come only from his loins. Tiziano had no doubt that Victoria was equally capable of overseeing a variety of stately homes, staffs, and all the rest of the nonsense that went along with a certain degree of consequence in some circles. She would go about it with blameless efficiency and a minimum of fuss, selecting the appropriate friends, activities, and boarding schools for whatever heirs she produced and then taking herself off to breed corgis or *take an interest* in the stables.

She was most assuredly not the sort who would take up with a string of lovers once her childbearing duties were dispatched. Not Victoria. She would dedicate herself to tedious charities and saintly volunteer opportunities, piously giving back while *setting an ex-*

ample as best she could. She was a paragon, raised to neither expect nor demand anything of the men in her life, while making a quiet sort of mark upon the world that would be remarked upon only in her obituary.

Even thinking about shackling himself to such a relentlessly irreproachable creature just about put Tiziano into a stupor.

Meanwhile, he knew a great many things about *this* woman who he still held in his grip, entirely too aware of the warmth of her skin against his palm.

"Did I ask you your name?" He knew he had not. "I'm certain I meant to."

She swallowed, then lifted her chin. And he took her in, the red hair curling so wildly that it defied the clips she'd attempted to use to tame it. Those gray, expressive eyes that marked her not as a paragon, but a woman of decided tempers.

Passion, something in him whispered.

"Annie," she said, with obvious reluctance. "My name is Annie Meeks. Sir. I take it you mean to report me?"

"I'm not going to report you," he assured her. And then, indulging an urge he could not have named, he tested her name on his tongue. "Annie."

This time, when she flushed, he knew it wasn't temper. And more, that it wasn't the sight of him that made her react that way. That it was this—her name in his mouth. Something personal to her. Something that wasn't intimate, by any means, but also wasn't the same, run-of-the-mill attraction every woman who crossed his path felt at the sight of him.

Tiziano fancied he felt something like it, too. And he was pleased it existed, he told himself. And better yet, that it was manageable.

Because Annie Meeks, run-of-the-mill secretary in the bowels of Accardi Industries, was in every possible way inappropriate. She was no gently bred aristocratic miss. Her broad vowels were coarse, and marked her as beneath him even if the obvious differences in their attire had not already done so. He suspected that one of his shoes could have bought her entire outfit. And whatever wardrobe went with it. Twenty times over.

"Thank you." Annie's tone was guarded. Her gray gaze searched his. "I wouldn't blame you if you did report me. I'd like to assure you that I hold both you and the company in the utmost respect—"

"That is enough now," Tiziano said with a dismissive laugh. "I'm not my brother. He is far more concerned with appearances. What is appropriate, what is not. If I were to claim that I was suddenly worried about such things that would mark me hypocrite, I fear."

She made a neutral sort of sound, still holding herself too still. Though he could feel a slight quiver within her, there beneath his hand.

He let his gaze move over her, remembering the hint of pink lace, the indentation at her waist. The echo of that liveliness in the temper he'd seen crack like lightning through the gray of her gaze. The rosy cheeks. The spray of freckles above her nose.

She would do.

In fact, she would do quite nicely, especially if she really did need her job. Or any job, really, which Tiziano supposed applied to most secretaries and all such people who were forced to work for their living. That meant she had a price. And, happily, he was nothing if not capable of paying it.

He could pay her far more handsomely than anything she was likely to get by filing tedious documents and answering to the phalanx of beige middle managers in this place.

Because he had an idea. The kind of idea that made him a marketing genius, if he said so himself. Only in this case, it was not the company that he would be marketing. But his own private life.

"I have a proposition for you," he said.

Her gray eyes narrowed. Once more, not quite the hosannas from on high he might have expected from another woman. But he liked the unfamiliar sting of it. "I'm honored," she said, and he could see that this was clearly a lie. She swallowed, then forced a smile that did not reach the outrage in her gaze. "But I must immediately decline any propositions. Mr. Accardi. Sir."

Tiziano let go of her elbow and stepped back, so he could lean against the wall and study her. And the more he looked at her, the more he was certain he'd found the answer to all of his problems. Particularly when she had her temper working. If he took her at face value, scuffed shoes and ill-fitting attempt to follow the corporate dress code, he could see her as one of these working girls who seemed to fill all the cities of the world—one indistinguishable from the next. There were veritable hordes of them traipsing about the Big Smoke, dreaming of getting on the property ladder, squeezing out a few whelps with some milksop lover, and then ascending to the dizzying heights of a semidetached in one of those indistinct English towns made mostly of cheerless bricks and the faint praise of middle-class ambitions. But if he squinted, he could see something else.

What he could make of her.

"What do you dream about, Annie Meeks?" he asked.

She blinked, her expression suspiciously bland. "A time machine. So I could go back and take the lift."

A beat, and then he laughed, and this time in sheer delight. "But you do not understand, *cara*. I must congratulate you, for your life has just changed." He paused, but she only continued to gaze at him balefully. He inclined his head. "It cannot possibly be your wish to toil away, unnoticed and unappreciated, forever. And indeed, you do not have to. Tell me what it is you dream of and I will make it happen. This I promise you."

"I really must have a concussion," she murmured.

Nothing about the way she looked at him softened. Surely he should not have found that compelling. "Because I might not be as sophisticated as some, but I hope I'm not foolish enough to imagine that something that appears too good to be true is anything but."

"For all you know this is an expression of my many eccentricities. Perhaps I trawl the abandoned halls and back stairs of Accardi Industries, bestowing goodwill upon whomever I pass."

"If you'll forgive me, I think we all know you do no such thing."

He laughed again, because she'd said that so sweetly, and yet he could see the truth of her feelings in her gaze. "I'm starting today."

"And what will you do with my dreams if I share them with you?" she asked, in a tone he could only call *challenging*. "Assuming I can remember any of them, that is. Fickle things, dreams. It's mostly those who can afford to indulge them who ponce about, worrying over them in the first place. The rest of us have work to do."

"What if I made it so you could afford to ponce about at will?" he countered. "Or anything else you like, for that matter?"

"And maybe tomorrow morning I'll wake up to find myself the Queen of England," she replied briskly. "But either way, that won't get these files sorted or my rent paid. So if you will please excuse me—"

"Annie," he said, liking the name more and more, each time he said it, "I want you to be my mistress."

He thought she might collapse, perhaps. Or smile knowingly. Maybe he expected her to do as another woman might and feign a great and theatric dismay. What he did not expect was the way her brows drew together, treating him once again to that ferocious scowl.

Tiziano liked it even better this time around.

She flushed once more, and he understood that he was seeing her temper again. A bright hot flare of it, unmistakable.

He liked that even more.

"Or you'll have me fired, is that it?" She laughed then, though it was a sharp sound and bitter besides. "No need, Mr. Accardi. I'll save you the trouble and quit."

Then she took the files she held and threw them on the floor. This time they didn't go up in a plume of fluttering papers. This time they made a loud bang, and even so, it was less furious than the way she looked at him.

She took a deep breath, and something gleamed in her gray eyes, putting him in mind of a set of talons. "And having quit, let me be clear. I think you are the most—"

"You mistake the matter, I think, *cara mia*," he interrupted, silkily. "You will be my mistress in name only, *chiaramente*. Or did you imagine that I, Tiziano

Accardi, who is often seen in the adoring company of princesses and international superstars, would lower myself to propositioning women for sex in sad office stairwells?"

CHAPTER TWO

ANNIE MEEKS HAD never been this close to a real, live billionaire before. Or really any powerful being, so drenched in privilege that he was *languid* about it.

But she had been to a zoo or two in her time and really, this was no different from standing at one of the big cat enclosures, watching a creature who should have been impossible slink about before her, all sleek and mesmerizing, as if to distract the unwary from the fangs.

She knew that was fanciful, at best. The reality was that Tiziano Accardi was no otherworldly jaguar, prowling about London, a creature of myth and legend.

He was a man. A man who was wearing hundreds of thousands of pounds worth of bespoke attire, which, like everything about him, was so obviously expensive that he could get away with wearing it all so carelessly. But he was a man despite all this.

He was also astonishing.

Annie had seen his face on a thousand tabloids,

like everyone else who drew breath. In pictures, the ethereal quality of his beauty was what came through. The operatic cheekbones. The sensual mouth. The contrast between all that and thick, dark hair that tousled about over moody blue eyes.

In person, however, there was that voice of his, like sin distilled into wonder. More worrying, there was a kind of brooding masculinity that poured off him, making her think less about the things that made him beautiful and more about those things that made him a man.

She had to remind herself, sharply, that gifted as he might have been in physical attributes, it was the gift of his particular genealogy that truly made him who and what he was. Generations of wealth and importance, handed down from parents to child again and again, so that it was no wonder he thought he was God's gift.

There was not a single thing in his life to indicate otherwise.

But that didn't explain what was happening here. Or the staggering thing he'd just said.

"I don't know what you normally do in stairwells," Annie found herself saying, which wasn't wise. Particularly in that tone of voice.

Then again, she'd quit her boring and yet stressful job here at Accardi Industries. And she would have to deal with that later and all the ramifications of it, she knew that. Truth was, she already regretted it. Annie was tempted to simply set off down the stairs and go right back to work, assuming—correctly, she was sure—that Tiziano Accardi could no more pick one secretary out of a pack than he could do his own washing up. He'd never worked a day in a job that wasn't granted to him by virtue of his surname. She doubted he even knew how to locate the lower levels of the building where the common folk toiled away.

But she'd given him her name, hadn't she?

She could feel the panic creep in, because scruples were all well and good, but they wouldn't do a thing to pay her debts. And well did she know it. Because if being honest and having scruples in the first place got a person ahead in this life, she'd be at Goldsmith's even now, studying for her art history degree. The way she'd been doing before her thoughtless, selfish sister had taken out all that credit in her name.

But she couldn't let herself think about Roxy. Not now. Not here in this very stairwell where she'd made a right mess of the lifeline she'd arranged to climb out of the hole her sister had put her in.

"It is true that I'm very versatile," Tiziano drawled, in an alarming manner. *Alarming* because she couldn't simply *hear* the man. She could *feel* that voice of his all over her, low and silken. "But alas, *cara*, ours must be a business arrangement."

Annie didn't know what was worse. The way he said that empty endearment, so *Italian* and so careless. Or the way he'd said her actual name before, which had made everything inside her…shiver.

She was still shivering, a fact that made her temper kick in.

"I don't understand this conversation and I don't want to," she said flatly, because she, by God, would *act* as if she was made of sterner stuff no matter what was quivering about inside her. "Here's what I do know. You are literally famous for being able to step into the street and have women attach themselves to your trouser leg before you've taken a step. There's no reason for you to be talking to me. About any kind of arrangement. Ever."

His surprising blue eyes—because surely a man so utterly Italian should have eyes like bitter coffee or melting chocolate or tiramisu of some kind— gleamed in a way she also felt *all over.* "But you see, that's why you're perfect."

There was something about the way he lounged there against the wall, as if his very spine was too lazy to support him otherwise. She knew that was the general take on Tiziano Accardi in all things— that he was only ever upright, and clothed rather than cavorting about in sensual undress, under protest.

But the look in those stormy blue eyes of his made her suspect that wasn't quite true.

"Perfect," Annie repeated flatly, ordering herself to ignore the man's *eyes*. He was an Accardi. An Accardi soul had no windows, unless they offered the most expensive view in any given city. "Why do I think that even if that's true, it's not a compliment?"

He lifted an indolent shoulder. "It appears you are remarkably suspicious, *cara*."

That endearment again. She couldn't say she cared for it. But that was the least of her concerns.

Annie knew exactly what she needed to do. It was glaringly obvious. All that was required of her was that she excuse herself, politely. Pick up the file folders once more, then march herself off to her supervisor's office. It wasn't ideal that Tiziano knew her name, certainly, but why did she imagine that he would remember it? Surely men like him saw a woman and had instant amnesia that any others existed or ever had.

That was likely to happen even more quickly in a case like this, surely, when it wasn't as if he'd noticed her. As a woman, that was. Instead of…whatever it was he was proposing.

She didn't have to know exactly what a man like him was proposing to her to know it was unflattering. Their relative positions in the world told her that without either one of them having to say a word.

There was no question about what she needed to do, and yet…

Deep inside her, she felt a long-dormant curiosity shake itself off. She'd packed it away with all the rest of the things that she'd so foolishly thought were hers, until Roxy had taken them from her, one by one. Dreams. Curiosity. An interest in the world around her. She'd put all such childish things behind her when she'd accepted reality, courtesy of her faceless bank and the notification of insufficient funds that had made no sense to her.

Until it had.

These days Annie kept her head down and her mind empty and told herself that was better. Much better, because the kind of person she was now, who budgeted down to her every penny, and would do so for the next three decades at least, didn't waste time dreaming herself silly.

These days she was practical. Distressingly so.

But there was a jaguar in the shape of a man lounging there before her in a bloody stairwell and there was that twisting, quivering sensation deep in her belly. And before she could talk herself out of it, or remind herself what was at stake here, she found herself tilting her head to one side in consideration. And even crossing her arms as she regarded him.

As if she had nothing to lose.

"Explain to me what you mean," she told him, less an invitation than a command, and she could see he found that amusing. Those moody eyes of his gleamed.

"My brother has taken it upon himself to reha-bilitate my tattered reputation," Tiziano said in that *voice* of his that no tabloid photo could have prepared her for. Expensive silk with a hint of some rougher edge that made her...too warm.

"A doomed enterprise, I would've thought," she retorted. Tartly.

The gleam in his eyes intensified. "Just so. But perhaps you have heard of my brother as well, and so realize that he cannot be told anything when he has made up his mind. Mountains are more malleable. And infinitely more pleasant."

"I can't say I'm familiar with either," Annie said with a sniff. "Not a typical feature of the lowly work I do, as it happens. No mountains or billionaire bosses lurking about. Just secretarial work, on command."

"What I notice, Annie, is that you sound as transported by your profession as I am by my brother's plans for me." He almost sounded like he meant that. That anything about them was at all similar. It didn't make sense. Especially when he smiled. "Surely if we join forces, we can help each other."

"There's no question that you could help me, if you deigned to do so," Annie pointed out with what her sister had once called her *relentless and unnecessary honesty*. Not that they talked any longer. "Just as there's no question that such help would inevitably come with strings. Nooses, I reckon."

"Nooses are little more than a necktie, unless you tighten them," Tiziano replied. "Though there are some who crave such things, of course. To each their own. Life is meant to be a banquet."

Annie ignored that, and not only because, in her experience, life was less a banquet and more a bit of cold, dry toast no amount of jam could disguise. "The real question is, what help do you imagine I could give you, and why do you imagine I would wish to give it?" She shook her head with more resolve than she felt, which should have scared her. "There are words for women who sell their services to men like you. But I expect you know that."

What she expected, really, was for him to take offense at that suggestion.

"You're thinking of words that are applied to lesser men, surely," Tiziano told her, those dark eyes dancing, clearly not the least bit offended. "When a man such as myself partakes of transactional relationships, an entirely different vocabulary is brought to bear. Many such women are known as *wives* to a man with a fortune, I think you'll find."

"To clarify," Annie said dryly, after a moment, "as romantic as this conversation is, you are not proposing marriage."

"Certainly not." There was a flash of that smile of his that she was distressed to discover affected her, no matter how many times she'd seen it splashed across the tabloid newspapers. Or even flashed about this very stairwell. "Though matrimony is at the heart of my current dilemma, it is not what I require of you."

"I see it's become a requirement. That's a bit fast, don't you think? Moments ago you were begging me for a favor. But not for sex in the stairwell, because you are you, the great and vainglorious Tiziano. I beg your pardon. I meant *glorious*, of course."

"*Certo.* Of course you did."

And then, for a moment, everything seemed to

collapse into that gleaming gaze of his and the way he looked at her, as if he, too, couldn't quite understand what it was he did here.

Annie was no expert on the man, or any man, but it almost looked to her as if he…caught himself up. He had the look of a man emerging from a dark interior into a sunny day. As if he didn't quite know what he was about.

She waited for him to make his excuses and swan off, back into his glittering life, but he didn't. He crossed his own arms, so they were facing each other now, mirroring each other's body language.

And Annie couldn't think of a single reason in all the world that she should feel something rather like *hot*, when it was the middle of a blustery November.

Tiziano considered her. "My brother feels that the rehabilitation he seeks for me can best be achieved by playing the sort of futile games our ancestors so enjoyed."

"Land acquisition? The callous disregard for serfs and slaves?"

His eyes gleamed again and he nodded faintly, as if to say, *point to you.* "Along those lines, yes. It's a tale as old as time. Find the most virtuous girl in all the land, renowned for her saintly works and unblemished innocence, and hand her over to a dissolute rake such as myself so that she might cure him. We've all heard that story before. We all know how it ends."

Annie sniffed. "Syphilis?"

He laughed, and she had the sense that he was as shocked by the sound as she was, as if it was no affectation on his part this time but an honest reaction. And again, there was no reason she should react to the things he said or did. He was nothing to her. Just an odd interlude with no bearing on the rest of her life.

"I assure you that my dissolution does not run quite so deep," he told her, his gaze and voice still ripe with that unsettling laughter. "Nonetheless, I find myself less than amenable to the idea of shackling myself to a paragon of virtue that my brother feels I should."

"Perhaps he should marry her," Annie said with a shrug. "If he's so taken with her."

"I have suggested the very same thing," Tiziano said. "Alas, no greater martyr has ever walked the planet than Ago Accardi. So despite the fact that the poor girl ticks every last box on my brother's wish list for a perfect bride, he has declared that she is for me. His unworthy younger brother, who can only be elevated by such a connection."

"Look," Annie said. "If I know anything in this life, it's that families are complicated." She knew better than to think of Roxy at a time like this. Or at all. Her sister made her far too upset, even now. She cleared her throat. "But no matter how tempting it might be, surely honesty is the best course."

"You do not know my brother." Tiziano sighed. "It is not that I don't understand him. I do. He had to grow up too fast when our father died. His whole life has been consumed with what he sees as his duty to the family legacy. I am the only stain upon his record, and he wishes to wash the record clean."

Annie blinked. "I didn't expect psychology from you, I have to say."

"I'm very complicated, *cara*," he said, with a grin that encouraged her to think he was lying. When she found it did the exact opposite. "But just because I understand my brother doesn't mean I wish to live my life with his foot upon my neck. Much less married to a woman who bores me silly. It's not her fault. She's lovely. Blameless in every way. And yet."

Annie told herself that was all catching up with her, careening into him, shooting off her mouth, and quitting the job she couldn't afford to lose. That was why she suddenly felt so…itchy. It had nothing to do with him waxing rhapsodic about a woman she didn't know and *he* clearly didn't even like.

"But meeting you has given me the key to this mess," he told her. He managed to give the impression of great flourish when all he did was *look* at her. "A mistress."

It was an archaic word. Annie told herself that was why it seemed to wind its way through her, like sensation. She made a show of impatience. "Again, surely you already have a battalion of women who could fill that position."

"I do," he agreed. "But we are not discussing what I might look for in a woman I wish to actually have such an arrangement with." One of his brows rose. "You see, do you not, the words we use when we speak of these arrangements. Far more civilized than what you were suggesting, I think."

"Wealth is always civilized," she agreed. "Because if you have the wealth you get to decide who's civilized and who's not. It's a snake eating its own tail kind of a thing."

"What I need is a woman wholly inappropriate for me," he said, and there was something so smooth, so silken about his delivery that it took Annie a moment to realize he was insulting her. And ignoring what she'd said. "A woman beneath my notice."

"Would that I was beneath your notice," she replied, and she could hear the edge in her voice. "I could even now be free of this conversation."

His mouth curved. "I'm not trying to insult you. I'm speaking only of how others will see such a connection."

"Because you are blind to class differences, I'm sure." She reminded herself that there was absolutely no need to fence words with this man. That could only prolong this interaction. "And I don't see how this would help you, anyway. So you date a secretary. Why on earth would anyone care? You date anything that moves."

"We will not be selling me *dating*," he replied, looking and sounding so unruffled he might as well have been half-asleep. It was maddening, she found. "We will be selling a mad, passionate love affair that

I will, of course, refuse to give up even should I agree to marry on command."

Something inside her jolted at that, in ways Annie did not care to excavate, but all she allowed herself was a sigh. "I would've said you were incapable of such a thing."

"That is my point."

And if she wasn't mistaken, the famously easygoing Tiziano had a temper, after all. She could see the flash of it in his blue eyes. If she was at all wise, she would beat a hasty retreat—but she didn't move. It was as if she'd forgotten how.

He went on. "If I were to come before my brother and declare that I'd fallen head over heels with one of the numerous interchangeable supermodels who follow me about from one party to the next, he would dismiss it. And carry right on with his plans. But if I present him with a woman like you, a woman entirely different from all who have come before, that will give him pause. It will be tempting to believe that the only reason I could make such a choice is the reason anyone acts so far out of character." When she only gazed back at him, he sighed. "Only the deepest, most passionate love, Annie."

"Sounds to me that you've been reading far too much Mills and Boon," Annie said dryly. "It's made you silly in the head."

His eyes were gleaming with amusement again, and she preferred that.

She opted not to ask herself why she was tallying

up *preferences* concerning the *jaguar* she was currently cooped up with. *Only no one is* cooping you up, she told herself sternly. *You can literally walk away at any time.*

Yet here she stood.

"It won't be a lifetime commitment," he continued in a dampening tone. "I imagine it will take no more than a week or two. Everyone wishes to announce the engagement at Christmas. I imagined that if I start banging on about how I refuse to give up the brand-new love of my life, my saintly intended will call it off before then. Or rather, her bulldog of a father will do the honors. We should both be back to our lives in short order." This time both brows rose, in an expression of breathtaking arrogance that, somehow, suited him. "Although if you agree, your life will be vastly and incalculably improved."

Annie frowned at him, because that shouldn't have been appealing, gift horses being what they were. And yet. "You don't know the first thing about my life."

"I know that if you were a woman of means, you would not be toiling away as a secretary."

Annie opened her mouth, prepared to mount an argument when she wasn't sure why she felt so compelled to argue in the first place, but he lifted an indolent hand.

"Think," he urged her quietly. Intently. Not without that arrogance, but with a kind of seriousness besides. "What do you have to lose?"

And despite herself, Annie did think.

There was a part of her that wanted to rail at him. To point out that for all he knew, she had a partner she adored and twelve lovely children waiting for her at home. But then, if she did, would she have lingered this long in a stairwell with a stranger?

The fact was, she had neither. Annie lived in a grotty bedsit in a questionable neighborhood, twenty minutes' brisk walk from the nearest Tube. Not that she bothered to walk to the Underground anyway, because saving every penny she could meant walking to work, though it took the better part of ninety minutes. In all weather. She ate tinned beans on toast more nights than not, washed her things in the sink, and rationed out her teabags.

She'd been scrimping and saving like this for a year now, and what did she have to show for it? Precious little movement on her debt, that's what.

And meanwhile Roxy had fled to Australia, where she could text her insincere apologies every now and again and carry on living as she pleased. Quite as if she hadn't ruined Annie's life.

It hardly seemed fair.

Also unfair was the simple truth that Annie had spent her whole life doing the *right* thing, not necessarily the easy thing or even the pleasurable thing. She'd gotten stellar marks at school. She'd worked hard for her place at university. She'd never given her poor aunt a single moment of worry, because surely the poor woman had enough on her plate, raising her dead sister's kids as her own. Annie had followed every rule. It had never occurred to her to act like her sister, so reckless, so ungrateful.

And what did she have to show for it? Roxy was living merrily Down Under, splitting her time between Sydney and Melbourne, or sunning herself on the beaches of Brisvegas. Annie was here. But even if Roxy hadn't helped herself to Annie's credit cards, Annie wouldn't be living *merrily*, would she?

She would be working toward her degree, congratulating herself for pursuing art history, which could be put to sensible use later. Rather than what she truly wanted to do in this life—because she'd decided long ago that it was irresponsible to risk throwing herself into her painting. Painting was almost certainly not going to pay any bills.

But if she took Tiziano up on this offer, she wouldn't have to worry about bills for a long time. Possibly not ever again. She could do what she liked. She could turn her grandmother's old cottage, locked up tight and neglected these last few years, into a studio and lose herself in oils and colors, canvas and daydreams...

Annie knew one thing without question. Her sister wouldn't have waited this long to say yes, as loudly as possible.

So what was holding her back?

Where had following the rules gotten her? She could decline this offer, but what would she have to show for it? It would take her years to dig her way out of the hole Roxy had left her in. Years upon years, just to get herself back to zero. At which point, there'd be nothing to do but start all over again.

Just once, she thought now, she should take the easy way and see what *that* was like. Just once, what if she threw caution to the wind like everyone else seemed to do with little to no repercussions?

She wouldn't be the first woman in the world to find a *transactional relationship*, as Tiziano had called it, appealing. There was a reason it was called the oldest profession, and if he meant what he said, he didn't even want the traditional form of payment.

Tiziano could have pressed his case, but he didn't. He stayed where he was, lounging before her, looking supremely unconcerned as she grappled with her conscience. And a few things that had nothing at all to do with her conscience, but should have.

She thought of her sister's last text, all *Xs* and *Os* and a picture of a sandy beach, as if that was supposed to stand in as some kind of consolation prize. And then:

It just got away from me. I didn't mean anything by it. Wish you were here.

Wish you were here, indeed.

The words seemed to echo inside her, growing heavy spikes and sticking in deep.

Maybe, just maybe, this was all a huge message

from above that what Annie needed to do was change, well, everything.

And there was no time like the present.

After all, how likely was it that a jaguar would escape from the zoo once—much less again, when she'd had more space and time to think through what he was offering?

"Very well, then," she told him, sounding dour and formal to her own ears, but he might as well know up front that she wasn't like the women he was normally draped in. That was meant to be the whole point. "I'll do it. But there will have to be rules. Boundaries. And penalties if those things are compromised."

She expected him to balk at that. Because surely he was used to the world turning to his specifications. And she had no idea what boundaries she ought to demand or what penalties she should require if he broke them, only that she couldn't simply *acquiesce*. Not without *some* backbone.

But Tiziano Accardi, who still reminded her far too much of an exotic and oversize cat, which wasn't good for her and was no way to begin a business proposition, only smiled.

CHAPTER THREE

IT WAS THE strangest moment of her life, including the terrible moment when she'd finally discovered what Roxy had been up to. Just like then, Annie stood still while the sense that everything was changing—might, in fact, already have changed—hurtled toward her at breakneck speed. And with no way out.

Only this time she was still standing in an Accardi Industries stairwell.

Whether that was better or worse than standing in an impersonal corporate bank location, facing the grim reality of skyrocketing debt she hadn't acquired yet was responsible for, she couldn't say.

Yet.

Tiziano smiled at her for what seemed like a very long time after she agreed to his proposition, making her instantly regret her choice. But not enough, somehow, to open her mouth and tell him she'd changed her mind. Not enough to do what she should have done from the start and just…keep walking down the stairs.

Eventually, he pulled his mobile from his pocket, typed something in, and then returned the full force of his sultry attention to her.

"Molto bene," he murmured. "My assistant will meet you and take down your many particulars. I will meet with my brother and begin making noises about the heart wanting what it wants and so on. That is the phrase, no?"

"It is *a* phrase," Annie said, surprised that she could speak when she couldn't seem to do anything else. Like leave. Or stop this thing even as she stood here watching it hurtle out of control. It was as if she'd hiked herself over a fence and taken a dive straight into one of the big cat enclosures at the zoo. Now it wasn't a question of *if* she would get eaten alive, only *when*. She cleared her throat and straightened out her spine. "If you're really trying to sell the idea that you've fallen suddenly and improbably in love, I might suggest that you look a little less cynical while you're about it."

Annie expected some fangs at that, but Tiziano only laughed, which did nothing for her composure. As she was contemplating that laughter, and the way light seemed to appear from nowhere and cascade all over his beautiful face while he did it, she heard the door on the landing above them open.

And maybe it wasn't a surprise that her first re-action was relief. Surely whoever turned up would restore some much-needed reality to…whatever this was. Annie would limp off back to her supervisor's office with the bruises she was surely developing, and by the time she settled in with her tinned beans this evening in front of her laptop, streaming programs so as not to pay the television license, she would think this had all been a bad dream.

Then again, she thought as he sobered, his face growing no less beautiful as his laughter faded, *perhaps not a* bad *dream, necessarily.*

There was the sound of heels against the steps and then a woman of indeterminate age appeared before them. She could have been anywhere between thirty and seventy, built sharp and slender, with the sort of long face and aggressively nondescript white-blond hair that—even ruthlessly contained in a sharp bun— made her resemble nothing so much as an Afghan hound. She marched down the steps, gimlet-eyed, until she stood beside Tiziano.

"This is Catriona," Tiziano announced, back to sounding lazy. "She handles my personal affairs, insofar as they require handling. I will leave you in her capable hands."

"Right," Annie said. "Because there are so many affairs, they really do need a manager."

Tiziano only laughed again. The woman beside him did not. Undeterred, Tiziano treated Annie to a sweeping, comprehensive study, from her head to her feet. So intent was he that she found herself flushing in response, as if he was actually reaching across the landing and putting his elegant hands on her.

Or maybe it was the rapid-fire Italian he launched

into, the lyrical language seeming to wind its way all over and even *into* Annie while Catriona nodded her sculpted blond head, typed busily away into her mobile, and murmured the occasional, *"Si, si...pronto."*

After what felt to Annie like a lifetime or three, Tiziano straightened from the wall. And when he looked at her then, those blue eyes of his seemed as unnaturally bright as the rest of him, and pierced straight through her. She felt pinned to the wall.

"Arrivederci, cara," he said, though it sounded less like a goodbye and more like a threat. *"Ci vediamo presto.* I will see you soon."

That was almost certainly a threat, or anyway, that was how her body reacted to it. She flushed from her hair to her toes, and the embarrassment of it made her blush even brighter, until she was fairly sure her skin matched her hair.

Tiziano only smiled again, this time in a way that made Annie's breath seem to...stop. A condition that did not improve when he turned and headed up the stairs in all his state, leaving her in his wake without the faintest idea how she'd let this all happen.

It was a lot how she imagined people must feel when they woke up blindly hungover with the attendant splitting headache and evidence of a night ill spent, a rite of passage she had managed to avoid thus far.

She swallowed hard, then turned to find Tiziano's assistant watching her, very closely, with absolutely no expression on her face.

This was Annie's chance to escape, now that Tiziano had taken himself off. His attention was like a tractor beam—she could admit that to herself, now he'd left—and it was time she did what she could to repair this situation. Meaning leave this building immediately and worry about her debt later, when—

"If you'll follow me," Catriona said, in a smooth, honey-toned accent that flirted with Received Pronunciation without actually making her sound *too much* like a BBC announcer. Though it was a close call. The BBC by way of Essex, to Annie's ear.

"Well," Annie said, as if she was hedging. As if she didn't know what she wanted to do. As if this was a debate. "I really shouldn't."

Catriona merely held out a slender arm and inclined her head toward the stairs, indicating that Annie should precede her.

Later, Annie was sure, she would think back to this moment and recognize it as the point of no return. After all, no matter how sleek, it was highly unlikely Tiziano's *assistant* was also a billionaire in her own right. Or any kind of uncaged predator, roaming the stairwells of London to scoop up the unwary.

Not that Annie was one of *the unwary*. What she was, she reminded herself then, was eternally neck-deep in the quicksand of Roxy's debt—and sinking. Unless she took this opportunity. Unless she acted completely out of character.

But then, what had acting *in* character done for her so far?

And then, before she knew it, she was walking up the stairs.

Catriona quickly proved herself to be an unstoppable force all her own. First she swept up the stairs just slightly behind Annie—not unlike a proper herding dog, Annie thought dryly—and ushered her into an office on the floor just below the executive level. She bid Annie take a seat in her office, which was all done up in elegant pastels, and then she proceeded to interrogate Annie. Over every last detail of her life.

Catriona left no stone unturned. She cracked open a laptop, input all of Annie's answers, and was not the least afraid to ask for further clarification. When she was done, Annie sat there on the dove gray settee, feeling rather like she was cracked wide open. Like a hopeless egg that could never be repaired.

Meanwhile, Catriona ignored her entirely and launched herself into a flurry of activity, sending out a barrage of emails and then making rounds upon rounds of calls. This meant that there was no opportunity for Annie to talk about second thoughts. Or even, really, to have them.

Later, after Annie signed stacks upon stacks of legal documents, Catriona led her out of the office without once looking up from her mobile phone as she typed out more messages, sprinting along in her high heels as if they were a cozy pair of trainers.

Annie had trouble keeping up and she was well aware that *she* wasn't the one with her face in a device.

"Mr. Accardi will have all your debts settled by

the close of business and an initial sum transferred into your bank account as a gesture of good faith," Catriona told her coolly as she strode along. "The contents of your flat will be boxed and transported and should be at your disposal by morning. Does that meet with your approval?"

Annie had been grateful that they were moving, charging down a hushed corridor as Catriona asked these questions and rattled off this information as if it was…something less than life-altering.

She felt something intense wash through her, so full-on that it nearly knocked her off her feet. This was all it took, in the end. All the struggle, all her work, all she'd given up—none of that mattered. Tiziano need only belt out a few instructions, this fearsomely poised woman had only to carry them out, and *poof.* Annie's worries were gone as if they had never been.

The whole thing, from falling on the landing to now, had taken less than an hour.

Less than sixty minutes to become a completely different person with a brand-new life, and she hadn't even gotten to the *mistress* part yet.

At the bank of lifts, Catriona paused and lifted a brow. Annie remembered that she needed to actually speak. That her *approval* was required. She managed to clear her throat.

"Yes," she said, aiming for sounding placid though her lips were numb. "That's fine."

And she must have lapsed into a kind of walking,

debt-free coma then, because later she would have no memory of exiting the building, or climbing in whatever vehicle was waiting for them. Annie only knew what was happening again when they arrived at what looked like a small museum in Hampstead, notable for its size, its odd crescent shape, its gleaming white exterior, and also the fact that it sat off the main road on its own acreage. Complete with a tennis court, a pool, enough glass to suggest the builder had meant to build the whole thing in a place like Mallorca to let in the kind of sun England lacked, and a sprawling sort of forecourt where cars—plural—could park.

Indeed, there were several obnoxiously sparkling sports cars of obvious pedigree sitting there already, parked *just so*, and beaming expensively in what little light remained of the mid-November afternoon.

"I would have imagined Tiziano as the sort for a flash flat in Central London," Annie observed before she had time to think better of it.

Catriona betrayed nothing on her smooth, unreadable face. "Mr. Accardi has several London properties."

Annie assumed that meant he *also* had a flash bachelor flat for his debauched purposes. She told herself it was a relief that he did, and that he hadn't had her brought there. For that likely meant he intended to go off and carry on with his usual behavior where she wouldn't have to see it, and wasn't that nice?

But it didn't feel nice, she discovered, as she

thought about it while the car they were in took its place in the shiny lineup. It didn't feel nice at all, and she couldn't have said why.

Catriona marched into the house—because it was, indeed, a house and not a museum. A house much bigger than the one where her bedsit was located, in fact. It was more the size of the whole block. Annie trailed along behind Tiziano's assistant, grateful that she could gape around at all the wealth on careless display rather than interrogate her feelings. About anything.

Inside, they were greeted by more staff, and everything became a whirl of directions, orders, and then, with an impatient jerk of her head, Catriona charged up the curved stairway that hugged one of walls that seemed to float about the place, giving way to the glass walls. Clearly Annie was meant to follow, and so she did, feeling more and more like the most egregious country mouse with every step.

Especially when she was marched down a hall into what was apparently its own *wing*, then shown into what was very clearly nothing more than one guest suite among many in this sprawling place. Still, it could easily fit her entire bedsit, times ten. She stopped walking as soon as she realized this, standing in what she thought was the main part of the suite, though it was hard to tell with all the posh glass and views over the Heath.

Annie suddenly realized she didn't know what to do with her hands. It seemed an odd thing to notice, but for a breath or two it was the only thing she could concentrate on.

"Welcome home," Catriona said in her unruffled way, managing to indicate that she noticed how ill at ease Annie was without *harping* on it, somehow. "Please take the rest of the day to settle in. A light tea will be brought up within the hour. If you'd like a supper later, all you need do is ring." She said that as if Annie should know what that meant, when all she actually knew was the sort of *ringing for servants* characters on period dramas did, but Annie nodded knowingly anyway. "Don't hesitate to ask for anything you might need."

Though Annie thought, when the door shut soundlessly and expensively behind her, leaving Annie alone in her *rooms* in bloody *Hampstead*, that the other woman rather hoped she *would* hesitate.

Not that there was any need to test the theory, because the *light tea* that was wheeled into her later would pass for an indulgent cream tea or two anywhere else. She had no need to *ring* for anything. The suite was equipped with three separate large-screen televisions set into walls and made to look like art installations. It had its own gym, a sauna, and balcony. There was an office, a study, and another room for no apparent reason. There were also shelves full of books in all these rooms—clever nonfiction, tedious business treatises, and quite a bit of fiction, too. Better still, there was a lake-sized bathtub with its own view across the Heath, and that was where

Annie spent her first night as a very rich man's supposed mistress. Lounging about in a glorious bath, outfitted with every possible indulgence, reading thick novels while she stuffed herself on finger sandwiches, petit fours, and decadent chocolates. Before taking herself off to a gloriously soft platform bed where she slept like a queen.

She rather thought she could get used to such luxurious splendor.

And yet the following week passed in far less indolence than that first night might have led her to expect.

Assuming that a person could really have any *expectations* about being swept up in the whirlwind that was the Tiziano Accardi experience, for which, apparently, he didn't even need to be present. That was just as well. If asked, Annie would have said that a man like Tiziano did very little at the best of times. Lounged about on this or that chaise, perhaps, forever awaiting the proverbial peeled grape, a nubile young woman, or ideally both.

But there were no nubile young women to be found in his overtly modern mansion in Hampstead. The house was filled with staff, none of whom seemed to be romantically inclined toward him, though all appeared rather unduly dedicated to the man. Many of them, she found as the days passed, had been with him since he was a child.

Some had even been with the family since his father was a child.

Annie had imagined she'd find a man like Tiziano surrounded by cynical staff, all champing at the bit to get out from service and away from their boss's antics. She found instead a vast house stuffed full of the sort of loyal family retainers she'd always personally believed were the province of a certain type of self-referential British fiction.

But it really did seem that none of the people who worked here were the least bit interested in changing their situation.

Maybe it wasn't that she found it surprising so much as she resented it. Because since she couldn't whip herself into a lather about the treatment of his underlings, she had no choice but to concentrate on the ways that *she* was expected to change. This was what Tiziano had bought when he'd thrown all that money her way. This was the transaction.

The first day or so were spent going through her meager belongings, which she was not permitted to do alone.

"Don't be silly," Catriona said when she arrived that first morning with the contents of Annie's bedsit in tow, then made it clear she intended to remain in all her faintly disapproving state. "I am trained to do these things."

What that meant, Annie discovered, was that Catriona ruthlessly divided Annie's possessions into two piles. One was of items that were to be packed away until her arrangement with Tiziano was over. That was the bulk of what little she had. The rest she was allowed to keep with her, though there were precious few of those and all of them personal keepsakes.

Her clothes were unacceptable, Catriona made clear. In every respect.

By this point, she'd slept in this house three times. The first night, the glory of the bath and the small fact that her debts were cleared had sent her off into a sound sleep. On the second, however, the silence kept waking her up. Jolting her to heart-pounding alertness as she kept sitting up in a panic, looking around to see why it was the London that ought to be carrying on outside had gone so preternaturally quiet.

The bed was too soft, that second night. The down in the pillows was too pokey.

Yesterday, she'd had two full days of having trays of food delivered to her whether she was hungry or not, endless cups of tea placed at her elbow, and Catriona's matter-of-fact approach to dividing her things. If that wasn't enough, Tiziano's blade of an assistant had then sat her down for a brisk recitation of debts cleared, monies allocated, and an overview of what had been sketched out for the trust Tiziano intended she use to follow those dreams he'd been banging on about in that stairwell. Plus more stacks of documents requiring her signature. It was all bloodless and overwhelming and she'd slept like a log.

So deep and so hard that when she'd woken up this morning, she'd had a dizzying moment of failing to recall precisely who she was. Much less *where* she was.

It stayed with her all morning, that feeling.

And it was not improved now. Catriona had herded her into a car after lunch, announcing that it was time to see to her woefully deficient wardrobe at last.

"I thought the point of all of this was that I was supposed to seem completely outside the normal realm of the kind of woman that man dates," Annie argued, perhaps a bit snappishly. "Wardrobe and all."

"There's a difference between the reality of a secretary and the public's Cinderella fantasies involving a secretary," Catriona informed her coolly as they were whisked off down the private lane. "We are going for the latter, Miss Meeks."

Annie had wanted nothing so much as to argue that, but she found herself curiously unable to say anything at all. She wanted to scream out that she hadn't signed up for any *Cinderella* stories, for God's sake. She wasn't the sort of person who believed in such tosh—not after the crash course in reality she'd had this last year. Besides, this was no fairy tale. This was all sleight of hand. All she had to do was loaf about looking mistressy and inappropriately northern, biding her time until Tiziano and his brother came to terms. She couldn't see how that should involve any particular effort on her part at all.

But Catriona was merely doing her job, and no matter if her manner was chillier than that of the average great white shark. There was no point arguing with her. Catriona was tasked with carrying out Tiziano's vision and Annie felt sure that somewhere in all the papers she'd signed, she'd agreed to go along with it, too.

And so, for the next few days, Annie simply... surrendered.

As much to the lashings of cream teas on command as Catriona's ruthless approach to shopping at what appeared to be every exclusive boutique in every upscale neighborhood in London. She subjected herself to climbing in and out of an endless array of clothes while Catriona wielded the credit card, and more, made the final decisions.

Nor was shopping all that was in store. Long after Annie had become numb to the astronomical prices, the casual condescension of the shop girls, and Catriona's blunt responses to outfits she didn't like, Catriona towed her off to a spa so exclusive that the staff all knew her name the moment she arrived. As if she was an old, dear friend.

"Welcome, Annie," they all said, in matching tones of obsequious delight, as if they'd known her from the cradle. "How lovely of you to drop in."

There was no checkout counter or product display in this spa, located in one of London's poshest neighborhoods, where Annie had never ventured. Nor had she ever found herself in a place like this, where there was no opportunity to so much as inquire after the price of anything. Why bother, when bottomless wealth was assumed?

The first day she was massaged and steamed, wrapped and packed in mud, which one attendant chirpily remarked was "getting London off your body."

What could Annie do but freefall into it?

And if she daydreamed a bit about stormy blue eyes in the face of a fallen angel, that was her business.

The next day, she was led straight back into the spa, but this time it was very plainly not about relaxation. This time, it was all about beautification.

She apparently needed a total overhaul, and her feelings on this were not taken into account. Her pride was not consulted at all. Her attendants smiled when she grumbled, but they had their orders.

Like Annie, they answered to the coldly efficient Catriona in all things.

Her hands and feet were tended to, nails buffed and polished. Hair she didn't even know was growing on her body was waxed away and/or shaped. And after a facial that had involved hot peels and exfoliants galore, her lashes and brows were tinted, with a bit of a lift to the lashes as well.

More procedures than she'd ever heard of were practiced all over her, and when they were all done, her hair was cut and quietly colored to enhance its natural shade, then blown out and styled to perfection. Instead of her usual mess of red curls, she now had a deeper copper gleam and suggestion of wild-ness, carefully arranged into sophisticated disarray.

Only when her hair was deemed suitable was she bustled into yet another part of the spa, where a host of technicians dressed all in black swirled around her, applying makeup with what seemed like trow-els. She braced herself. Because sooner or later she was going to have to look at their work and try her best not to recoil.

But when they all stepped away and presented her to herself in a room of mirrors, Annie was a bit disappointed—in herself—that she felt so...awed.

Because she saw at once what Catriona had meant about the public's fantasy of a Cinderella secretary and what they'd done here to realize it. Annie looked like *herself.* It wasn't as if anyone who'd known her for her whole life would no longer recognize her. And yet, at the same time, it was as if every part of her *glowed.*

As if the work they did at this spa was inside out.

Annie couldn't get over it. It was as if her own private sun shined down upon her, bathing her in the sparkle of her very own gold. The way a similar light had found Tiziano in that stairwell, transforming him into something far more dangerous than just a man.

She studied her reflection, trying to figure out what the shift was. The many treatments, sure, but she thought she ought to be able to tell exactly what was different. When she was wearing the sort of outfit she'd worn as a uniform at Accardi Industries. A pencil skirt. A blouse. Heels.

But though Annie would have said that she hadn't the faintest idea how to tell the difference between one item of clothing and the next, even she could tell that the clothes she wore now bore no resemblance to the ones Catriona had ordered packed off into boxes to be stored in some attic. It was the quiet, stately elegance of the fabrics, perhaps. It was the way they whispered against her skin, and the way the shoes, though high and surely structurally unsound, felt instead as if she were standing there in cozy bedroom slippers.

There was the hint of gold at her neck, the kiss of pearls at her ears.

She saw exactly what Catriona—and, she supposed, Tiziano—was going for. She looked fresh-faced, bright, and as filled with understated elegance as the clothes she wore. A modern-day working girl's Cinderella, in other words.

A masterpiece by any measure.

Damn it all.

Annie turned to face the other woman, who stood in the corner, her arms crossed, looking—it had to be said—unduly pleased with her handiwork. It was the most expressive she'd ever been in Annie's presence, and Annie couldn't help feeling as if that were a bit personal.

"I thought you were mad," Annie said quietly. "But even I can see the miracles you worked here."

The other woman inclined her head in her typically cool fashion, but there was the faintest hint of a flush of pleasure on her face. "No miracles required," she replied in her usual smooth way. "But I do take pride in realizing Mr. Accardi's vision."

And though there was no further personal talk, if that even counted as personal talk in the first place, Annie felt buoyed by the conversation. It was as if she and Catriona had come to a meeting of the minds.

She had almost forgotten that the point of all of this was not Catriona at all.

The point was the man all of this was for.

Annie had gone out of her way not to think about him over these last few days. Despite sleeping in his house, dreaming of him, and waking in a bed he owned. Then spending days preparing herself. For his pleasure.

Like some barbaric virgin sacrifice, after all.

She told herself, briskly, not to be dramatic. After all, hadn't he made it clear that he wanted no part of her body? Not in that way?

You know he did, she told herself tartly, once Catriona dropped her off that evening. Leaving her to walk, unattended and better dressed than she'd ever been before, to walk down a winding, cobbled street toward the restaurant where she was to meet up with Tiziano at last.

She told herself that she was glad he'd made himself so clear the day they'd met. That she was *delighted* a man like him wanted nothing to do with her, not really. And that as they played this elaborate game of pretend, she would have the opportunity to know, up close and personal, that men like him were exactly as vile as she'd always supposed.

Annie kept telling herself that with every click of her heels against the hushed, expensive street, where she never would have come of her own volition. She hadn't even known there was a restaurant here, she thought, not that she spent her time cataloging swank restaurants in posh Central London neighborhoods.

But then, that was because the likes of her weren't *meant* to know there was a restaurant here. There was no mark upon the door. It was merely an address to what looked like a converted old Georgian house. She half expected that when the door opened at her arrival, it would be Tiziano standing there, welcoming her into one of his numerous London properties.

Instead, she found herself ushered swiftly through the lushly appointed house to a private room. The smiling, yet distant, butler—or that was what she assumed the man was—swung open the door and waved her in.

And finally, Annie saw him again.

Tiziano Accardi, who was not a figment of her imagination, bolstered into something impossible over the past week because she'd been immersed in *preparing herself* for him. To be his mistress, if only in name.

If anything, he was *more* astonishingly beautiful, seductively masculine, than she remembered.

He stood by a set of French doors that opened to the garden below, looking out. Though she knew in an instant that he was fully aware of her presence, he waited for the door to close before he turned.

His gaze found hers, the blue of whole seas Annie had never seen with her own eyes.

But she could see him.

And she could feel the immensity of him fill the room they stood in, making her feel small—but in a way that only made her want to marvel at him. To celebrate the difference in their positions.

It was in that moment that Annie realized, with a certain sinking sensation, that she had completely underestimated the situation she found herself in.

CHAPTER FOUR

TIZIANO WAS PREPARED for Annie to look well. To look irresistible, yet unexpected. That was what his assistant had been told to achieve and he already knew that Catriona had spared no expense.

But *looking well* in no way described the woman who stood before him.

The woman he'd met in that stairwell, red-haired and gray-eyed, had been pretty enough, in her way. He could admit to himself that had she not been, he would never have propositioned her as he had. He was who he was, after all.

Yet the woman before him tonight made something deep within him still.

She was luminous. She looked almost ethereal, and it took almost everything he had to stay over by the windows when everything in him demanded he cross to her. And better yet, sink his hands into all that thick, red-gold hair. He wanted to wrap it around his fists, then hold her so he could plunder that wide, generous mouth at will.

He wanted to trail his way down the length of her body, dressed to perfection in a body-hugging skirt that made her curves nothing short of a national treasure. He wanted to press his mouth to the pale honey of her skin until he'd tasted every inch.

God help him but his sex was heavy, and the need for her so intense, that he had a moment of something far too close to panic as he wondered whether he would be *able* to keep his hands to himself.

As if he was no more than some heedless boy, hopped up on hormones.

The silence dragged out between them, and he knew that it was happening. But he seemed to have no access whatsoever to the charm that had always served him so well until now.

He rather felt as if someone had dealt him a stinging blow to the head. There was a ringing in his ears and his heart pounded, only making the need in him wind tighter and tighter.

"I'm sorry if the dress-up doll you ordered is not to your taste," Annie said tartly then, with that broad hint of the north shaping her words. And his weakness had always been beauty, packaged to drive men wild. He hadn't realized that all of his experiences had been lacking *this*. This kick. This tartness that made his mouth water.

Her.

"You'll do," he replied.

And realized only after he'd said it that he'd done

it just to make her eyes flash like that. Because he basked in it. He wanted to do it again and again.

Instead, he crossed to her, taking her arm solicitously and leading her to the table. He seated her before the fire with great formality, then took the chair opposite.

Annie looked around, taking in the quiet, unobtrusive elegance of their surroundings. "I can't tell if this is a private house or restaurant."

"A little of both, I suppose," Tiziano replied, absurdly let down that she wished to discuss...the *place*. "It's more a kind of club. Where gentlemen of certain social strata have been entertaining women for centuries."

She seemed almost to relax at that, though her eyes glittered. "Mistresses. You mean mistresses, don't you? Not wives. Or any women auditioning for a ring, for that matter."

"Certainly not," Tiziano agreed, and was pleased to note he'd located his grin again. At last. "This is England. In Italy, these things were more fluid. They still are, because expectations are different. But in London, clubs like this exist so that men of a particular station might leave their duty at the door and cater to their true wants and needs within."

"I wouldn't have thought you cared about privacy."

"The point of this evening, Annie, is not the privacy. It is not what goes on here. It is what will happen when we leave."

"Will I be chased down an alleyway by a pack of baying paparazzi, then?" She wrinkled her nose, as if imagining such a scene. As if Tiziano was the starlet du jour, who could expect such treatment during her fifteen minutes of fame. "That's one of the perks of your existence, by all accounts. I can't say it holds any appeal."

"There will be no packs and no chases in alleys." Tiziano leaned back in his chair. "This is not that sort of establishment, because the paparazzi know that if they take pictures of those who frequent this place, they will not get the other pictures they truly want that will sell their tabloids. Still, there are those who lurk in the shadows and make note of who comes and who goes anyway. They might not take a photograph, but they like to know who's in play." He inclined his head. "You can consider it a soft opening for your new position."

Then he sat back, enjoying himself far more than he should have as the staff came in with their meal, when this should have been no more than another tedious business meeting. Annie was far more captivating than she had any right to be.

He took pleasure in her artlessness. Her reaction to the presentation of the meal, and then, as if that were not mesmerizing enough, her clear delight in every bite of the food, which he knew to be reliably excellent. But he had never been here with a woman who acted as if each and every bite was a revelation.

As if she thought the point of being here was the food, not the company.

Perhaps that was truly why he was captivated, he found himself thinking later, as their rich, decadent dessert was cleared away and they were left with tiny cups of strong coffee.

He was not sure he had ever made it through an entire meal here before. Normally, he would expect to be deep inside his companion by now, food forgotten, as they both took their pleasure as they could.

Tiziano did not know how to process the strange notion that he found a different kind of pleasure in this woman. In how fully she threw herself into every bite she took or gave herself over to every sip.

He couldn't tell if he had never known, or if he had only forgotten, that pleasures could be so uncomplicated. That there was a beauty in the simplicity of joy. And he found himself fascinated by this woman who had seemed so bristling, so armored, when he'd met her. Yet now appeared to think nothing of showing him her every last reaction to the delights of a fine meal.

Stranger by far was how deeply he enjoyed her reactions.

So unstudied. So *real*. It made him wonder when he had last experienced anything quite so authentic.

If he ever had—or if that, too, was something that had died in his childhood.

But he did not like to think of such things.

"I trust you are enjoying the house in Hampstead,"

he found himself saying into the silence, because another thing that set Annie apart was that she made no effort whatsoever to draw him out. She did not *attempt* to captivate him in any way.

Left to her own devices, he was forced to conclude, she would sit in perfect silence here. She would enjoy her food, not caring in the slightest if a single word was ever spoken between them.

It was not that he found this *refreshing*. That was not the right word. But it was a novelty, and he found himself longing to explore it. To explore her. He hadn't been thinking of such things this whole week. He'd been laying the groundwork with his brother and preparing to wage his little war before Ago acted like a feudal lord and made declarations about Tiziano's future for all the world to hear.

He hadn't expected to be knocked sideways by the sight of his little secretary, all dressed up as his mistress.

But since the sort of exploration he craved was not advisable under these circumstances—for reasons he was certain he would recall in due course—he settled on making conversation.

"It's a lovely house, isn't it," she was saying, which he knew by now was not a question, coming from the English. "Lovely people working there, too. To be honest, I'm a bit surprised."

"That I own a house? I do not know how to tell you, *cara*, that my real estate portfolio is varied and vast."

"That you inspire loyalty," she retorted. And he saw it again then. The girl he'd first met in that stairwell, in a shower of documents. It was there in her eyes and the spark of it seemed to glow in him, too. "Not what you're known for, I would have said."

"I do hate to disappoint you."

"I wouldn't say it's a disappointment." But then, while he watched, interested despite himself, her cheeks reddened. "Right." She sat up straighter. "Tell me how you think this is going to go. This whole mistress game."

"I'm not going to tell you everything." He offered her a disarming smile, though he wasn't sure it worked the way it was meant to. Not on Annie. "Your natural reactions are part of the point."

"Because you want an overawed country mouse, I assume." And he was certain he could hear whole moors in her voice just then. The wuthering wind and all.

"Only some of the time," Tiziano assured her. "As for the rest, well. After tonight, we will endeavor to be caught out."

Her gray gaze was steady. "Caught out where?"

"There will be any number of tedious, interchangeable events," Tiziano said with a bored sort of shrug. "But this game of ours will rise and fall on how swept away we are by each other. How heedless we become in public. That sort of thing."

That gray stare did not so much as waver. "How heedless do you imagine we will become?"

"Exceedingly heedless."

And then, following an urge that he should have quelled, he leaned in closer. Because she was not like the other women he knew, and the point of making her his mistress was not to treat her as if she was.

He knew that. Truly he did.

He knew it, but he couldn't seem to make himself behave.

"Shall we practice?" he found himself asking, even though he knew he shouldn't.

Tiziano expected her to draw back. To haul off and hit him, or even storm from the room. Because this was most certainly not what they'd agreed upon. Or maybe it was, because he did like to put on a good show, but he'd intended to ease into that part.

But she did none of the things he expected her to do. Instead, she propped her elbows on the table and rested her chin on her hands. Her head canted slightly to the right as she regarded him.

"If you mean a kiss," she said, as if she'd given the matter a great deal of thought, and Tiziano was not prepared for the way that notion rebounded in his sex, "then I suppose we'd better."

Once again, he found he had to remind himself that he was no green, spot-faced whelp. Nor ever had been.

The way his body reacted to her statement, anyone might have been forgiven for confusing the issue. He took a moment to study her, to calculate the best way forward when he couldn't quite trust his own reactions.

He knew a great deal about Annie Meeks by now. The exhaustive questionnaire that his assistant had administered covered all possible areas, doing away with the necessity of any sort of question and answer between them.

It was not necessary for him to ask her where she came from, for he knew. She had been raised in the north, in one of those Yorkshire towns that had once been little more than a textile mill, all dark bricks and gloom. Her parents had been killed in a boating accident when she and her sister were young, leaving them in the care of an aunt. There had been a grandmother, doting by all accounts, but she had died some years back. The sister, three years younger than Annie, had decamped to Australia some eighteen months ago, after what appeared to be extreme dedication to partying. Annie, by contrast, had spent her gap year interning at an art museum in Leeds while working as a waitress on the side. She'd spent her fresher year at a college here in London in an art history program, but had quit her education to take up her secretarial job at Accardi Industries.

But he knew more than that. He knew that her sister had stolen at least one credit card and Annie's identity, too. He knew she'd racked up enormous debt in Annie's name. Or rather, the sort of debt a woman like Annie would consider enormous. That was what he'd paid off this week.

Beyond all these facts, he knew her romantic history as well. Such as it was.

He studied the picture she made before him now, glowing softly in the candlelight. She was even more beautiful than he could have imagined, and he could admit that after he'd seen her crawling around on the floor before him, he'd done some imagining. Tonight she looked far more sophisticated than she had then, yet there was also an air of innocence about her no one who saw her would be able to resist.

Tiziano was banking on it.

What he had not expected was that he would fall prey to it, too.

He'd expected the report from Catriona to come back with the expected teenage boyfriend or two. Then a bit of experimentation, for wasn't that the purpose of university? He had greatly enjoyed the women of Cambridge in his years there. The report, however, had indicated that this woman who was to act as mistress to one of the most dissolute men in Europe, by his own reckoning, was innocent.

Almost entirely.

Save for a few kisses, Annie Meeks was largely untouched.

Tonight, gazing at her beauty before him, he found this unfathomable.

Not least because it meant that he couldn't haul her up against him, hold her to the wall, and ease that ache in his sex the way he'd like to do.

And he really couldn't recall the last time he'd felt the slightest inclination to practice *restraint*.

"Or maybe we shouldn't practice kissing," Annie said, which made him realize he'd been gazing at her for some time, letting the silence between them stretch out. "Though I will say, I was under the impression there was scarcely a lass in five continents who you *wouldn't* get off with, given the slightest provocation."

"I do have some standards," Tiziano replied, with a laugh, though he couldn't decide if he wasn't the smallest bit offended. He, who took offense to nothing. "Some would say I have the highest standards imaginable."

Her smile was placating. "Did someone actually say that to you? Out loud?"

Tiziano stood, smoothing his hand down the front of the suit he wore. He was aware it wasn't a necessary gesture. Unless his aim was to direct the attention of his companion to an abdomen that he knew, quite objectively, was stupendous.

Maybe he was *preening* for this woman.

Annie followed the movement of his hand, then raised her gaze back to his. "I'd have thought that a man as comfortable putting yourself about as you are wouldn't be afraid of a little kiss."

The dossiers he had his assistant prepare had always seemed sufficient, before. But Annie was different. He didn't care about the facts of her life, not when what he really wished was that he could read her. Because he couldn't. Her gray eyes might as well have been a bank of thick fog for all he could see through them. He had no idea what she might be thinking.

And when had he ever been in the slightest doubt about what went through the female head in his vicinity?

But not this female.

Not Annie.

"I was under the impression that you hadn't done enough kissing to call yourself an expert," he said, mildly enough.

He wasn't sure what reaction he expected, but it wasn't the way she laughed, and not the way the women he knew usually did. Not that tinkling bit of laughter, as if they were trying to sound like bells gently ringing. This was a bawdy laugh. The kind of laugh that would turn heads in a restaurant, causing those who heard it to find it either shocking or infectious.

Tiziano found it a bit of both.

Because it lit him up. It seemed to move inside him, as if the sound of her laughter was kicking down doors he hadn't known were closed within him.

He felt something like...dazed. Or possibly intoxicated.

"I've seen pictures of you," she told him. "I couldn't have avoided them if I wanted to. Sometimes there's kissing and sometimes there's not, but the last thing I want is to look like is a fool in photographs the whole world will be looking at. Better safe than sorry, I always say."

"Not always," he found himself replying, with something less than his usual careless ease. "Or I doubt you would be here."

Annie laughed again, but she was pushing back her chair and rising to her feet. And he had miscalculated, because as entranced as he might have been by the curves he'd seen in that stairwell, and that bit of pink lace he still carried around in his head, he hadn't been adequately prepared for the sight of those curves in clothes cut to flatter them. Eating a meal with her had lulled him a bit, it seemed. It had made him forget.

She was...lush. There was no other word that fit. Annie had the sort of proportions that made men silly. Across the ages, across cultures, an hourglass shape such as the one before him now inspired the male of the species to go a little light-headed. Their hands itched to carve out that shape in the air between them, to see if the curves before them matched.

It was past time, Tiziano told himself sternly, that he attempted to get hold of this *hunger* that was making him so restless. Clearly, it was a function of his having announced he didn't intend to bed her. He was so unused to restriction that the very hint of it drove him to distraction.

He lifted his hand, then beckoned her close with two fingers.

Languidly.

And told himself that his low, intense heartbeat then was merely his body's way of congratulating him on a job well done in choosing a woman so unlike his usual fare. A woman who was certain to captivate the world, if only because she was so unexpected. Not at all who people expected to see on his arm. They wouldn't be able to look away from her. They would believe, almost without meaning to, that he'd fallen head over heels in love with her on sight—for who could not?

He was not considered a marketing genius for nothing.

Annie moved closer. Then she stood there, gazing up at him, and it was only then that he could see some hint of what might be going on beneath her surface. The tinge of pink on her cheeks, the faint widening of those gray eyes.

It roared in him like triumph.

"One kiss," he said, and he meant to sound sophisticated and possibly even bored, so he could not have said why it was his voice came out so...raspy. "For practice, that is all."

It did not help when she shivered, delicately, and then tried to hide it. Possibly failing to realize that he could see the way her nipples tightened behind her soft blouse.

Tiziano gritted his teeth. Then he stopped, and made himself smile.

"Come closer," he told her. Gruffly.

"Said the spider to the fly," she replied. She laughed again, only this time it was less that surprisingly full-throated expression of joy. This time it was much more uncertain.

It was a good reminder, and Tiziano took it. He reminded himself that while he surely was no one's idea of a saint, that didn't mean he couldn't attempt to play the part. Since it suited his plan here. Besides, being careful with her was certain to infuse their public outings with a lovely sense of him *doting* upon her in a way he never had before. Not with any of his other women.

And it would make them seem even more convincing.

He reached over and slid his hands to her face, cupping it between his palms. She was wearing much higher shoes than she had been when they'd met, and he liked, very much, the height they gave her. They put her at just the right angle so that he only needed to bend down a reasonable amount to put his face near hers.

And then, aware that she was regarding him solemnly with those rain-soaked eyes of hers, Tiziano pressed his mouth to hers.

Rather formally, really.

He was certain he had never kissed a woman so *delicately* before in all his days. But Annie was not just any woman, and this kiss was not about him. Therefore, he did not indulge that darker, beating thing within him that wanted only to pull her closer.

To wrap his arms around her and press her lushness against him. He did not deepen the kiss the way he would have at any other time, to get a taste of her and drive them both wild.

Instead, he kept it *saintly*. Chaste and easy.

The kind of kiss that would look lovely when it was splashed across a front page somewhere.

But what Tiziano was not prepared for was the *ache*.

The kick of a kind of eroticism he was wholly unfamiliar with. For he was not indulging it. He was not chasing it. It was the simple fact of their lips, pressed together. It was the warmth and the feel of her.

To his astonishment, his body responded as if he was already deep inside her.

Tiziano kissed her like that a moment more, then pulled back. He was shocked to find his heart still beating wildly, that ache inside him so heavy and intense it was a wonder he could see straight.

He dropped his hands and smiled at her. He thought to himself, *extremis malis, extrema remedia*. Because in this case, the game he played was worth this attempt to make himself into some kind of martyr.

Why not smile while he was at it?

Tiziano was therefore completely unprepared when all she did was blink a few times. She pressed her lips together, as if tasting them, which should have been sultry…save for the expression on her face.

It took him some moments to comprehend that

Annie Meeks, of late a secretary, really was looking at him as if she had just had...a less than ideal experience.

A less than *transformative* moment in his arms.

"Well," she said, in the bright sort of tone that one uses when trying to make the best of a bad situation, "that's a bit of a letdown, isn't it?"

"I beg your pardon."

It was not a question. He was not begging. He was...flabbergasted. A *letdown*?

"I've been kissed before, of course," she told him, in a confidential sort of manner that made him want to throw the table they'd sat at out the window. As if he was a common brawler. "It was all very much the same old thing. You know, very run-of-the-mill. Lips upon lips, and if you think about that—about what it *is*—it's not very appealing, is it? But I did hope..." She flapped a hand at him. The way he had once seen a woman in the country flap a hand at her *chickens*. "What with all the hue and cry about Tiziano Accardi, the greatest lover of his generation—"

"I see you have read widely, indeed."

"It's just that I thought it would be *exciting*," she said.

And the mad part was that she sounded almost philosophical. As if she'd given it a try, and she appreciated him doing his best, bless him, but in the end was disappointed.

Disappointed, by God.

It was unsupportable.

Tiziano acted without thought. He moved toward her again, hooking his hand around the nape of her neck and hauling her toward him. And he took a great pleasure in the way her body thudded into his, all of her lushness suddenly *right there.*

He anchored her against him with his hand in the small of her back, pressing her where he wanted her and enjoying too well the high-pitched little sound she made in the back of her throat.

Without worrying about his impending sainthood or tabloid photography or any social niceties of any kind, he bent and claimed her mouth.

The way he'd wanted to all along.

And this kiss was pure fire.

Tiziano licked his way into her mouth. He angled his head, drawing her closer, so that he could taste her and tease her, tempt her and beguile her, every time his tongue slid against hers.

He kissed her again and again, shifting position so he could sink his hands into all that red-gold hair at last. And still he kissed her, until that beating thing in him was so loud he was certain that she could hear it, too. That all of London could hear it. He kissed her until she was quivering in his arms, her body soft against his, her breath coming hard and high.

Tiziano kissed her until she was weak in his arms and then he kissed her more, until he thought it was possible that they would both taste nothing but each other for days to come.

Months, even.

And only when he was on the very brink of throwing her down to the floor and coming down after her, wild and greedy to fully claim her as *his*, did he stop.

Though it cost him.

He set her away from him, and his self-control—which some might have thought no more than a myth—had never before been so tested.

It hung by the barest thread.

But he held her upright until she looked around, flushed and flustered. She swallowed hard, seeming to struggle to find her balance. Only then did she step away, putting the necessary distance between them—not that it did any good.

Her taste was in his mouth. And the need for her was in his sex, like a shout.

Annie stared at him, but despite the clamor inside him, he took it as a victory. Because this time, she seemed to have no commentary whatsoever. Her eyes were huge—and he could read them clear enough.

Especially when she lifted a trembling hand, pressing the pads of her fingers to her own lips.

If he was a better man, a saint or a martyr, he might not have taken such satisfaction in this.

Luckily, Tiziano had never *truly* pretended to be anything of the kind for more than a few moments. Right here in this room.

He made himself smile, though he had never felt less like smiling in his life. But he had been playing his role for a long, long time, so he trotted it out, forcing himself to relax. Languid and unconcerned, because that was who Tiziano Accardi was and always would be.

It was critical that this woman, above all others, know it well.

Because, whispered a little voice inside him, *this woman is the first you have ever met who might threaten it.*

He shoved that thought aside.

"Tiziano..." she whispered, but barely. As if his name was a curse. Or perhaps, more tempting still, some kind of prayer.

He did not wish to be tempted. Not by this woman. It was an outrage.

But all he did was incline his head. "I trust you have no further concerns about my ability to sell a decent kiss, Annie."

The hand at her mouth dropped to her side and her gaze followed, and Tiziano had no earthly idea why he should feel those things like some kind of loss. As if she'd taken them from him. When she lifted her gaze again, that unreadable mask of hers was back and he could not help but resent it.

Though it was clear to him that he should not. That he should not care in the slightest.

"I think it should be perfectly adequate," she told him. "For our purposes."

Adequate. The *insult* of it all.

Her voice was bland. Her gaze, even more so.

Tiziano did not for one second mistake that for the challenge it really was.

"I'm delighted you approve," he murmured.

And it took far more effort than it should have to make himself appear as unbothered as he usually was—and about everything. He took against it. And her.

Hard.

Tiziano's smile then was languid, but the way Annie stood straighter, he was sure she could see the light of battle in his gaze. He did little to hide it. "And do not worry, *cara*. I doubt your need for practice shows. Much."

CHAPTER FIVE

KISSING TIZIANO WAS a terrible mistake.

And not because he had clearly agreed that she needed practice—something she should never have said to him. Annie knew immediately that she shouldn't have taunted the man. She didn't know why she had. That simple kiss had been bad enough. She'd no idea what devil it was that had wormed its way inside her, making her challenge him the way she did.

It hadn't been a wildly passionate initial kiss, even she could tell that. But still, a press of Tiziano's lips to hers had wiped out any memories she might have had of her teenage years, where she'd gotten a kiss here or there. Never anything serious.

Yet it had all been embarrassing in comparison to the simple mastery of Tiziano's mouth on hers.

And the thing was, she really had done a lot of reading. There was no reading about Tiziano Accardi, tabloid darling, without all those *pictures*. And so she'd seen him nuzzling up to countless stunning women, looking lazy and satisfied, like a smug cat. All of those pictures had seemed to her far more tempting and treacherous and *serious* than that first kiss he'd bestowed upon her tonight.

Which wasn't to say she hadn't felt it.

She'd felt it *everywhere*, that firm mouth pressed against hers. And maybe because of that, because she could tell it was a simple little kiss when she knew he was capable of so much more, it was as if she couldn't help herself. She'd been forced—*compelled*, even— to push him.

Three days later, she was still reeling.

That night had ended shortly after their kiss, which was a great blessing, to her mind. She was surprised that she was capable of speech. Or thought. Or any motor function at all, come to that. He'd ushered her out of the little house, then bundled her into one of his sleek sports cars, all while seeming to hang on her—acting more attentive than she'd ever seen him.

Tiziano playing the besotted lover, she assumed. And even though she knew full well it was an act, it was shockingly effective. Her breath caught. His intent focus made her...melt.

That was a maddening thing about this man. Everything he did was effective, when he presented himself as anything but.

"Were we spotted as you hoped?" she asked with excessive politeness as he drove them through London, controlling the powerful car as easily as he controlled her. A thought that made something in her seem to shake apart.

"I'm certain we were seen, yes," he replied, in a manner that made her wonder if he'd seen to it himself. He slid a look her way at a traffic light, then returned his attention to the road. *This was a good start.*

And he hadn't spoken the rest of the drive to Hampstead. Once there, he escorted her to the door of his own house and executed a sort of half bow that should have looked absurd in this modern age—but, somehow, did not, because of the *Tiziano* of it all. Then he turned and strode back to the gleaming car and drove away.

No doubt off to entertain himself in his usual fashion, she had told herself stoutly. And wasn't it a delight that she was not cooped up in some flat with him while he entertained his many women?

Yet she couldn't even work up any temper over it, and not because it wasn't her place. But because the only thing she could think about was that kiss.

The *real* kiss. The kiss that had been any number of kisses, one after the next, hot and breathless and impossibly wild.

She thought of little else for days.

Three days, in fact, night and day alike, until she found herself waiting for him in the excruciatingly spartan foyer of what she assumed was the very bachelor flat she had been glad to avoid. Catriona had handed her off to a set of attendants who, the other woman said, would be responsible for all of Annie's *evening looks* from here on out. Given that it had not been evening at the time, Annie had been confused.

But it had taken the women who'd set up shop in her suite whole hours to prepare her for the dress she wore, an inky blue that hugged her shoulders and drooped just slightly in front—then swept down to expose the whole of her back.

If she exhaled too hard, Annie was fairly certain she might show her arse.

Then don't exhale, pet, retorted one of her attendants, with the sound of Hull in her voice. It made Annie feel a bit homesick, but in a good way.

It helped her remember who she was, and she needed that, because she saw no sign of herself in this creation her attendants had made. There was the impossible dream of a dress. But her hair was twisted up into something breathtakingly complicated, too, a mess of braids and twists that somehow all smoothed together to give the impression of a sort of bohemian sophistication that should not have been possible. Her eyes were smoky and mysterious, something she could see in the giant mirror across from her in this minimalistic foyer, where, if she wasn't careful, she would forget who she was looking at and surprise herself anew.

Annie blew out a breath and ordered herself to stop thinking about his open mouth on hers, the way his tongue had taunted her, drawing her out, sending all of that delirious heat crawling around and around inside her—

A faint noise made her jolt and her head whipped around.

And it was as if she'd conjured him out of the air.

Tiziano stood there, everything about him brooding and dark, save that blue gaze.

She dreamed about that color blue. That specific shade. It was as if it haunted her.

"What on earth are you doing in my foyer?" he asked in that haughty sort of amazement that he wielded far too easily. And too well.

"Waiting for you." And though all kinds of butterflies were wheeling around inside her, she was pleased that she sounded calm. Or calm enough.

"You're playing the role of my mistress, not my maid." There was that glittering thing in his gaze again then. And a kind of tightness in the air between them that made her belly feel hollow. "Mistresses do not lurk about in foyers like the help, *cara.* I thought perhaps you'd been struck down in traffic, only to discover you were dropped off a quarter of an hour ago."

"I wouldn't call it *dropped off,*" she argued. "They had to smuggle me in. It was like a kidnapping. They flung coats over my head and hustled me in through the service entrance."

"Does the glamorous life not suit you?" His voice was a smooth weapon. "A pity. It is considered the height of fashion to sneak in and out of buildings, concealing your identity and keeping your where-abouts mysterious."

"Is this because of the tabloids?" Annie made a face. "It seems a bit odd, doesn't it, that for all your money and all your power you're still at the mercy of a scrum of men who hang about in the street."

He gazed at her. "My company is generally held to be more than enough recompense for any indignities suffered in the service entrance."

Annie wished then that she hadn't stayed seated when she'd caught sight of him. She felt like a schoolgirl. But she thought that if she leaped up now, she would look even more foolish. Instead, she folded her hands in her lap and smiled at him.

Perhaps a little patronizingly, if she was honest. Because he'd earned it. "I'm sure your company is a tremendous lure," she said in an encouraging way that suggested she thought no such thing. It was worth it for the way his astonished blue eyes widened. "It's just that you could buy yourself the lot of them, couldn't you? I have to wonder why you don't."

He only stared at her as if he wasn't quite certain what shape she'd taken, right here before his eyes, and she took that as encouragement.

"It's one thing if you're an actor or some such. You need the publicity. But you are an Accardi. You already have everything you could possibly need, and then some. So I can only assume you enjoy the silly games of hide-and-seek, or surely you could just go ahead and buy yourself whatever agency hires these people. And fire them."

He blinked, more than once. That was all the reaction she got, but she congratulated herself all the same.

"You have already spent more time these past few moments thinking about the paparazzi than I ever have," he told her, back to sounding something indolent and authoritative at once. "It is not necessary to always sneak in and out of service entrances. I only do so when I wish to control the narrative." His brows rose, and he seemed to look down upon her from a far greater height than his six feet and then some. "Because it is my narrative, *cara*. This you must know above all else. It is my story, and it will always be told the way I wish it to be."

"Right," she said briskly. "You are a master storyteller. Noted."

She thought that there was something heavy, there in the air between them, but in the next moment he laughed, and it was gone.

Though, for the first time, Annie wondered what story his laughter was meant to tell.

"Come," he said, sounding as lazy as he ever did. As if she had made all of this up, the tension and the *storytelling* and even the layers she'd thought she'd seen in him here, for a moment. "This time we will exit through the front door. There will no doubt be a gauntlet of flashbulbs for you to navigate. The trick is never to look at anyone directly, no matter what they might say, or how they call your name. Or you will find yourself blinded and confused, and they will pounce."

"This gets better and better," Annie said brightly. She stood up then, and found herself smoothing down her gown, though it didn't need the attention. When she looked up again, Tiziano looked almost… stricken.

But she must have been mistaken. This was Tiziano Accardi, the man of a thousand lovers, and in any case, she was no more than an employee. Something she would do well to remember, she told herself sternly, when he put a hand to her back and guided her from his flat.

This is not a date. He is not treating me in this fashion because he has any designs on me whatsoever. Annie kept repeating that to herself, especially when the private elevator delivered them to the lobby. That, too, was kitted out in enough glass that all she could see was the jostling throng of people already waiting outside.

"'Once more unto the breach,'" Tiziano murmured, but all Annie could concentrate on was the feel of his palm in the small of her back. His flesh against hers. The heat of his palm, and the shivery sensation that radiated from that point of contact, until even her knees felt weak.

But there was no time to indulge *sensation*, of all things. Instead, she had to walk out into that baying crowd at Tiziano's side, doing her best not to fall off the skyscraper high heels she wore or betray too much anxiety to the watching horde outside.

She didn't realize how much the thick glass doors were muffling the intensity of the crowd until the doorman opened them wide and Tiziano led her into the thick of it.

It was chaos. It was terrifying. If Tiziano hadn't kept hold of her, Annie would have stopped dead as the wall of noise hit her and then turned to run back inside. She wouldn't have thought twice. It felt animalistic, the wild urge to put as much distance between her and all these harsh voices as possible.

And the voices were secondary to the lights. The *pop-pop-pop* of the lights, like weapons. It took her long, spinning moments to remember what Tiziano had told her. Not to look at them directly. To keep her gaze away from those constant flashes of lights.

It was too late, of course. Annie felt blinded and fractured and had no choice but to rely entirely on the man who guided her smoothly enough to the car that waited for them at the curb.

She slid inside and then realized in a panic that Tiziano was sliding in right behind her, so she had to heave herself across the leather seat toward the far side of the vehicle. All that noise was cut off, abruptly, by the slamming of the door, but then they started batting at the windows and the sides of the car.

It took her a long while to even notice she was holding her breath.

The car pulled out from the curb, slowly, but Annie was unable to move, or breathe, or even process what had just occurred. She thought, then, in that same spinning sort of panic, about all the tabloid magazines she'd seen in her lifetime. All those pictures. Had they all been taken like this? People hunted down in this way? It was nothing short of horrifying.

"Indeed," Tiziano rumbled from beside her, and it wasn't as if she'd forgotten he was there. He was not forgettable in any way. But she was startled to hear him all the same. It seemed to take an enormous amount of willpower to turn her head, and then to look at him. And even more to understand that she must have spoken out loud. "I have not paid these things much attention in a long while. I fear it is true that a person can get used to anything."

Annie swallowed, hard. Without meaning to, she lifted her hand and placed it over her heart, not surprised to feel the drumbeat there, a panicked staccato. "What I can't imagine is courting that kind of attention. It seems nightmarish to me."

Tiziano's dark expression was lightened in no way at all by the blue of his eyes. "Attention is currency, *cara*. My family is wealthy, *sicuramente*. But the perception of the Accardi wealth far outstrips our actual holdings." His mouth curved. "For surely there could be no playboy so disreputable as I, unless there was a vast fortune behind it."

"You could also be above such games." But even as she spoke, Annie could feel her whole body flooding with a kind of relief. As if she really had been under attack and was only now processing the fact that she'd survived. "Not every rich person appears in the tabloids."

"There are arguments for and against. My brother would prefer that the Accardi name never appear in print, unless that print is on the next round of contracts. But then, many of the contracts we enjoy have come to us because of the very profile I maintain that he so detests."

Tiziano shrugged all of that away, as if it was nothing.

Annie wanted nothing so much as to delve into the Accardi family dynamics. But that seemed a risky endeavor at best. For one thing, she couldn't really see this man opening up in any real way. And did she really want him to? She wasn't doing this because she wanted to make him a friend. She was doing this because it was as if she'd somehow won the National Lottery. For once, she intended to bask in her good fortune. If it involved flashbulbs in the face and three long hours to get ready to go out, that seemed a very small price to pay.

She smiled at him. As professionally as she could, given the circumstances. "I was told we were going to some kind of premiere."

He waved a hand. "Some film," he said carelessly. "When you invest in cinema, they do not call you a shareholder, you understand. They call you a producer and the honor of seeing your name on the screen is considered more than enough payment for some. Depending on the investment, of course. I am, obviously, a great patron of the arts—"

"In that you like to date actresses?"

His eyes gleamed. "Just so. They invite me to the premieres. As an investment opportunity or because they think my ego demands it, who can say?"

"Does that mean…?"

"There will be all manner of famous people about tonight?" He laughed, that warm, rich sound that filled the car and made her remember, too vividly, the feel of his palm against the flesh of her back. "I did not think you cared about such things. I should warn you now that you will lose any wonder you might hold for famous people before we're done."

"Including you?" she dared to ask.

And her reward was the way his mouth curved into a ghost of a smile. "Me most of all."

"I was a little more concerned about walking a red carpet," she said after a breathless moment and too much deep blue in her head. "I've never been all that interested in famous people."

"Aside from me, of course. Of whom you have read so much and so widely."

Annie sniffed. "I thought that was a job requirement."

And later, when she lay in her bed on its high platform, there in her room of glass, what she remembered was not the paparazzi. Nor even the supposedly more legitimate press corps who shouted

Tiziano's name as he walked her down the carpet, which was indeed bright red. It was not the film they watched. She couldn't recall a single scene, because all she could seem to focus on was the man sitting beside her and the brooding intensity of him in the dark. It was not even the party they'd gone to afterward, where every face before her was one she recognized from her telly or the supermarket checkout line.

All of that she filed away, but what she remembered most was the two of them cocooned in that car, gliding through the London streets, his laughter all over her like heat.

It kept her awake well into the night.

The good news was that the job of pretending she was Tiziano Accardi's mistress took place at night. No matter how late they stayed out, very often past dawn, nothing was expected of her until the next afternoon.

"I don't think I fully understood that what famous people are, really, are vampires," she said one night as she sat wrapped up in a dream of a cashmere scarf turned elegant blanket in the car, so delirious that she couldn't tell if she was falling asleep or perhaps already lost to dreamland.

Tiziano's voice hinted at all that dark laughter that lived in him, and she could feel it inside her, too. "In more ways than you know."

The job itself did not include the more physical duties a typical mistress might expect to undertake.

That meant Annie could have been as lazy as she wished. For the first week or so, she was. But after only that single week of excessive luxury, with cream teas wheeled to her at the snap of her fingers, it became clear that she needed to take better care of herself. Not only because she otherwise might need a new outrageously overpriced wardrobe, but because all that laziness made her peevish and strange.

If she couldn't work or study or paint the way she had once upon time, she could at least *move*. There were various rooms throughout the sprawling house, outfitted with various kinds of exercise equipment. One of those trendy stationary bikes. Various rowers, one shaped like a wooden bow and others stripped down to so many efficient parts. There was a weight room equipped with intimidating machines and racks of hand weights, all gleaming invitingly. There were treadmills on every floor and the gardens outside should the British late November ease its cold, grim grip.

But Annie found she liked the pool best. Because there were no mirrors or staff about to watch her. Because she could dive beneath the water, always kept precisely at the most perfect temperature, and simply swim.

And because swimming made her think, not of Tiziano Accardi for once, but trips to the seaside she and Roxy had taken when they were small. When their parents were still alive. When they would hire a caravan, eat tinned meat sandwiches on cold beaches, and shiver in the inevitable summer rain. Both girls had learned how to swim at one of their parents' favorite holiday parks.

While she was swimming, it was easy to remember only the good things. She and Roxy tucked into bunk beds, giggling late into the summer night. Chasing each other up and down the stretch of gray beach, pretending they might at any moment swim for Denmark. Their grandmother coming for a few nights to tell them stories about mermaids singing to the boats in the North Sea and selkies sunning themselves on the rocks.

Annie could remember, almost, her mother's calm voice as she read to them on the little sofa in the long summer evenings. She and Roxy would take a place on either side of her, a shoulder each, while their eyes grew heavy and their sticky fingers seemed to adhere to their own cheeks.

She remembered her father teaching his girls to dance, propping each of them on his feet as he moved around what little space there was inside the caravan while Mum fried up the sausages and the wireless played happy songs.

Annie still knew all the words.

And she sang them to herself as she swam in that pool, with the late November weather sometimes bucketing down against the glass outside. Her heart would leap happily inside her chest as she cut through the water, swimming end to end, over and over. And once she'd sung herself everything she knew, she started over again, until she found her way back to calm.

Because that serenity was what she prized, she realized. It was what made the difference.

Her input was not required in any of the other things she was called upon to do. Her outfits were chosen for her. Her *looks* were decided on by her team of attendants, and her thoughts on them were never requested. Sometimes it all made her feel a bit claustrophobic, stuck in a chair with so many people buzzing around her as if she were nothing more than a mannequin. But the more she swam, the calmer she felt in the pool as well as in the chair, and the better she could enjoy her afternoons being transformed into the perfect Accardi mistress. Because those afternoons were the calm before the storm.

The storm was Tiziano, thunder and heat.

And his plan was working just the way he'd intended it should.

At first, the pictures were of him—and her elbow, perhaps. Sometimes with a throwaway reference to his "friend." Or his "female companion," if they were feeling saucy. No one asked her name, and although there were always shouting matches beneath the bright lights, Tiziano did not furnish it.

But as the two weeks he'd expected rolled into three, and November gave way to December, he started taking her out to restaurants. All of them extraordinary, exclusive, and different from the club where they'd met that first night only in that there were other people in attendance. Or other people she could *see*, anyway.

That week, the tabloids were filled with pictures of the two of them looking intimate by candlelight, or walking out of exclusive restaurants in London neighborhoods she had never dared set foot in on her own, for surely there was an income prerequisite for breathing such rarefied air.

Who is Tiziano's mystery woman? the papers demanded.

Wild theories abounded online. But it wasn't until an art opening that first week in December that she began to understand exactly what Tiziano was doing.

The night started the way all her nights did. She presented herself to her attendants in the chair that now occupied that bonus room in her guest suite, that was, itself, now a mere extension of her newly vast wardrobe. By now she knew to appear in a shirt that buttoned down the front, and a pair of easy tracksuit bottoms. Not that either of those items were any less exquisite than everything else in her wardrobe, courtesy of Catriona. She was styled to an inch of her life, packaged in the gown du jour, and then swept off in a car to be delivered to Tiziano.

This particular night, the car had pulled up outside Accardi Industries. She'd spent a few moments wondering if she would have to parade into the office where she'd worked as a secretary dressed up like the belle of the ball.

Though even as she thought such a thing, she

laughed at herself. Because who would recognize her? Her supervisor had never looked north of her chest. And none of the other secretaries she'd encountered would look twice at a woman dressed as she was now. It would never occur to them that they could know her.

But she didn't have to put that to the test because Tiziano slid into the car, flashing her a grin that seemed to take in the whole of the sleek gown she wore and every inch of her exposed skin. As if his fingers moved all over her.

She sometimes wished they would.

Annie felt herself flush, and worse, felt the blue of his gaze, as if he knew exactly the sort of thoughts that had been plaguing her more and more lately.

If so, he said nothing. Sometimes, they would sit together in these vehicles of his and he would indulge himself in what she liked to consider his teasing. He would ask her questions designed to embarrass her. They were always probing. And inappropriate. At first, she'd taken great offense—until she realized that he meant her to.

But he wasn't the only one who could play games, and so once she made that determination, Annie made it her solemn duty to respond to each and every query of his with the same equanimity.

"Is it embarrassing to have that accent?" he might ask, lazily.

She would smile in return. "No more embarrassing than having more money than sense, I wager."

Most of the time, when they arrived at these events, they were both a little wound up from the battle that had just occurred in the car. She could see it on their faces in the pictures that turned up each morning. In what appeared to be every tabloid in every country across the globe.

Though it took her longer than she wanted to admit to figure out that the point of it was the pictures. Because it made them look like they'd engaged in a far different battle in the car.

Tonight, he took her to dinner and then to an art gallery, where he tucked her arm into his, and leaned too close as he led her from one piece to the next. He murmured for her ears only, his mouth so near to her she felt electrified by his breath against the side of her face.

And she knew it was for show. She knew that Tiziano was only playing a part. But it was hard to remember that it was all the same bit of theater when he was so good at it.

"Don't react," he told her while standing before a painting of a great, oblong object that shot from the earth to pierce the sky. "But I know the artist and I am quite certain that is a *highly* exaggerated rendering of his most prized possession." He looked down at her, his blue eyes gleaming too bright. "*Excessively* exaggerated, according to all accounts."

And Annie wasn't pretending to laugh when he was outrageous, she was really laughing. Just like she didn't need to pretend to be interested in all the rest of the things he said to her, because she truly was. He knew a shocking amount, not only about the artists' private lives and their favored appendages, but about their work. About art in general and how it mattered more than ever these days.

More astonishing still was that he actually listened when she told him her own thoughts and opinions.

He listened the way other men made love, Annie found herself thinking. And it followed, then, that he must make love the way other men made art—

But she couldn't indulge that line of thinking. Not here. Not with so many eyes upon them and her tendency toward a blush at the least convenient moments.

They'd been going round and round for some minutes now, standing before a canvas they disagreed on. He thought it was trite, she thought it was subversive, and Annie only gradually became aware of someone else standing in her peripheral vision as they argued the point.

She turned automatically—and found herself caught immediately in a stormy blue gaze she recognized.

Except this was not Tiziano, wreathed in easy grins and oozing languid insolence. She knew at once that this could only be his intimidating brother, the stern and disapproving Ago.

And tonight, it appeared he intended to share that

disapproval equally between his younger brother...
and her.

"What is the meaning of this?" he demanded.

Tiziano pulled Annie close into his side, and
though he laughed as he looked down at her, there
was a certain coldness in his gaze that hadn't been
there before.

"My brother wishes to chastise me," he told her,
and she understood that he was not speaking to her,
though he appeared to address her. "But if that was
all he wished, he would do it in Italian. That he is
speaking in English, you understand, is a way to
signal to you that you ought to feel shame in my
presence."

"Doesn't every woman feel shame in your presence?" Annie asked, without thinking. "I thought
that was the entire point of you."

Ago shifted position and frowned as if Annie had
managed to surprise him. What she couldn't tell was
whether it was her accent or her irreverence.

But Tiziano smiled, and it reached his eyes. "Afterward, perhaps," he murmured. "Not usually *during*."

His brother swept to look up and down the pair
of them, and focused his attention on Tiziano. "You
know that your fiancée is here, I trust," he said
coldly.

It wasn't as if Tiziano had hidden anything from
her. Annie knew that the purpose of the game they
played here was to save him from the altar. He'd told

her all about the worthy creature his brother had chosen to domesticate him. She'd looked Victoria Cameron up herself. But it had never really occurred to her before now that Victoria was a living, breathing woman who might, for all Annie knew, have a host of feelings about Tiziano. Why else would she have agreed to marry him?

How had that not occurred to her before now?

"I do not recall proposing to anyone," Tiziano was saying, mildly enough.

But looking back and forth between the brothers— both of them so tall, so dark, so elegantly ferocious, each in his different way—Annie had no trouble seeing that Tiziano was not in any way as languid as he was acting.

If anything, he looked more furious than Ago did.

Not outwardly. Never *outwardly*. But surely his own brother should have been able to see it, too.

If he did, Ago gave no sign. "All the arrangements have been made with her father. As you know well." He shifted his cold gaze to Annie and inclined his head, but slightly. "If this is news to you, I regret it."

"I don't think that you do," Tiziano replied, almost cheerfully.

Yet Annie could see he was anything but cheerful.

"I told you not three hours ago that tonight was to be the first glimpse of you and Miss Cameron in public," Ago bit off. "Was I unclear?"

"And I told you, not three hours ago, that I have no

intention whatsoever of playing this game of yours," Tiziano returned.

Once again, Ago looked directly at Annie. "My brother is using you," he told her coldly. "He uses every woman he comes across, I fear, but it is you he is using most egregiously. For he knows well that it is time he did his duty. And that is not you, Miss Meeks. I fear it will never be you. I hope he has not told you otherwise."

Annie wished that she had prepared for this. That she had some sort of script that she could fall back on, because all she could do in the face of Ago Accardi's obvious fury was gape at him.

Beside her, she could feel Tiziano coil, as if he was *only just* holding himself back from swinging on his brother. Right here in the middle of a posh, absurdly upmarket art gallery that seemed to be filled with even more famous people than that film premiere.

But Tiziano did not get violent. Instead, he pulled Annie even closer to his side, almost as if he meant to shield her. "If you have something to say, brother, you say it to me. I told you already. Annie is nonnegotiable."

At that, Ago scowled. He turned that scowl on Annie, but only briefly, before aiming it back at Tiziano.

"I told you," Tiziano said, his voice low, as if that scowl was a shout. "Again and again, I have told you. I will not give her up. This is not up for discussion.

Yet the great and powerful Ago Accardi hears only what he wants to hear. And has a magical deafness when it comes to anything I might say. I am used to it." And the way he glared at his brother should have turned Ago to stone. "But I will not have you vent your spleen on the woman I love."

And Annie knew that he was playing his role. *She knew it.* She had signed all those contracts. She had walked out of her life and straight onto this stage.

But knowing that didn't help. It did nothing at all to keep that electric bolt of sensation from coursing through her, a wildfire of need and longing, at the sound of Tiziano Accardi saying he loved her.

No matter how little he meant it.

Well, she thought then. *That's not good.*

CHAPTER SIX

TIZIANO FELT THE jolt go through Annie, and he wanted nothing more than to explore it, chase after it—but not with his brother looking on.

He had planned for this moment. He had known it would happen tonight. He'd sat in his brother's office earlier, subjecting himself to one of the lectures that had been increasing in frequency and *sturm und drang* of late, knowing that this art opening would offer the best opportunity to flaunt his mistress directly at Ago and the Camerons. No more containing his behavior to the tabloids, and Ago could take it up with Everard Cameron himself if the old man had a problem with it.

As Tiziano very much hoped he would.

But now it was happening, and it was different from how he had imagined it.

Because he didn't much care what Ago thought or what Everard Cameron was doing. All he found he could think about was protecting Annie.

Tiziano didn't know when *that* had started. He

was not, by nature, a protective man. Not for him the doting on others that seemed to occupy so much of some people's time.

He and his brother had been taught to consider these things a weakness. Why dote on anyone? What mattered was duty.

But even if he hadn't been raised to acknowledge and flout his own duty, he could not comprehend why he had such urges toward a woman he employed. Perhaps he did not pay her a salary, but then, he had always been significantly more old-school than people tended to believe, given how flamboyantly modern he made himself out to be when it suited him. The bottom line was that it made far more sense to him to house her and dress her and call her his mistress than to simply pay rent on a flat, as he knew some men did, and move various women in and out as his ardor cooled.

Possibly, having never done either before, he was treating Annie less like a run-of-the-mill mistress and more like a favorite. The way a notorious ancestor of his had treated an opera singer of some notoriety back in Venice in the 1800s, happy to leave his wife and children to rusticate in the country until he was forced to make appearances. Always against his will.

Tiziano found he understood.

Because everything would be going swimmingly if it weren't for these *feelings* inside him that he could hardly make any sense of. If it weren't for the way her shoulders fit so neatly in the curve of his arm, so that he was assaulted by her delicate scent each time he inhaled.

It made him wish he was a different man. The man he was pretending to be, in fact. It made him want to *do things*. And not the things he was normally associated with.

He was not surprised when his brother let out a short laugh.

He was equally stunned.

"'In love?'" Ago repeated, in tones of disbelief. "You. Tiziano. *In love?* I doubt very much you know the meaning of the word."

"Come now, brother," Tiziano said, sounding lazy out of habit when the truth was, he was far more focused on that faint shivering thing he could still feel running through Annie's lush little body. "Surely you do not wish to put your own ignorance of emotion on display like this. It hardly speaks well of you."

And then, before Ago could respond as he surely would, Tiziano stepped away. He steered Annie away from his brother, away from this conversation, *away* from this danger he'd put her in. He headed into the crowd, where he could engage in easy, pointless society conversations that did not involve him making any kind of declarations whatsoever.

But he did not remove his arm around Annie's shoulders. He told himself it was all about maintaining this fantasy that he was selling. He of all people knew how important that was. This was his show, after all.

Eventually, they moved away from the main part of the gallery and found their way to one of the tall café tables that had been set about the glassed-in atrium, while delicate foods and all manner of drinks were passed regularly by out-of-work West End actors. There was no need to hold on to her at a table. Obviously he released her.

But Tiziano was forced to admit that he had a hard time losing that contact with her.

A much harder time than he wanted to admit, even to himself.

Even if there was something to be said about standing close beside her, angling his body so that it was as if they stood there all alone. He, who had always preferred the bright company of the many, discovered that he wished it really was only the two of them.

"Your brother is rather fearsome up close," Annie said softly, cupping her glass of wine in a manner Tiziano could only describe as grateful. As if she thought it was saving her from him.

There is no saving you, he wanted to tell her, and not because it was part of the role he played.

"He has cultivated his fearsomeness," Tiziano assured her. "When we were boys, he was perfectly normal. It is only over time that he has had every inch of humor drained from him, as if he sprung a leak."

Annie took a sip of her wine, and only then looked at him in her gray, steady way that made everything go still inside him. As if he were the one with those tremors moving deep within.

"What happened?" she asked. "To drain him?"

Tiziano was too caught up in her gaze for his usual deflections. "He became boring, as too many members of my family have done in their time," he said, offhandedly, though he didn't produce a smile the way he usually did when he said such things. "It is a terrible affliction. You will find it crops up everywhere."

She didn't laugh. Her gaze didn't even lighten. Instead, he saw the suggestion of a frown begin in that wrinkle between her brows. "What does he think happened?"

"Ah. Well."

And Tiziano knew that they were standing in the middle of a bustling art gallery. That Ago himself was likely watching them at this very moment. He knew that the glare of so much attention was no time or place for confidences. He couldn't recall the last time he'd had the occasion to share any personal details with anyone. Not real ones.

He only shared stories that made him look even more disreputable than he was.

But there was something about the way Annie looked at him. As if she was silently, almost hopefully, encouraging him to be...

Not different, but *better*.

It should have irritated him. Instead, it made Tiziano wish for things he knew too well were impossible. He had picked his role long ago. For Ago could only be the avenging angel when there was a convenient devil forever at hand.

"Ago is the eldest son," he found himself saying, simply enough. And though that was true, and as comprehensive a way to explain his brother as any, something about the way Annie waited pushed him to go on. When he never spoke of these things. "And in a family like ours, despite what he may have wished or wanted, Ago was required to have a head for the business from a very young age. The Accardi legacy, you understand, is all that matters. He was encouraged to take part in pursuits that were carefully arranged to suit the business, and his future. If it did not serve the legacy, it was not for him."

Memories Tiziano had not aired in years pressed in on him, but he pushed them away. He and Ago had not been young in a long while. And they had been permitted their freedom, their happiness, for so few years. What good was it to recall such things now?

"It might surprise you to learn when he was young, Ago fancied himself a bit of an artist, after a fashion," Tiziano heard himself tell her. When he had never told another soul such a thing. It was not that it was a secret, or even his, but that it was painful. For too soon had they both been hauled out of the sweetness of art and childhood and taught instead how to make money. The only thing any member of his family truly believed in.

"Is that why we're here tonight?" Annie asked. "This is his gallery, is it not?"

Tiziano smiled. "He owns it, but do not lapse off into any artistic daydreams, *cara*. Owning a gallery is not romantic. It is the opposite." He shook his head, and wished she was still snug beneath his arm. And since when was he a man of *wishes*? "The art and romance was quickly beaten out of my brother. All the hopes and dreams of the entire Accardi Empire were placed upon his shoulders and he, being dutiful and good, widened his shoulders. The better to hold them all. He is the heir. The legacy was in his hands."

Another woman might have rushed in to say something. Anything. To express outrage that a boy should be molded so young, perhaps. Or make some crack about how Tiziano had missed out on similar guidance.

Annie only eyed him a moment. "And what was put on your shoulders?"

For no reason at all that he could comprehend, Tiziano smiled. But it was a bitter thing. And it seemed connected to all those memories he refused to entertain.

"Nothing at all," he told her with a soft ferocity that sounded nothing like him. Or more like him than he allowed outside his own head. "Air, if that. I was abandoned to my own devices—and vices—and encouraged to stay out of everyone's way. I was the spare, you understand, but there was no real concern that I would ever be called upon to take Ago's place. And thank goodness, as it was quickly determined that I would be useless in such a role."

"And so you decided instead to be outrageous." And Tiziano found himself mesmerized by the way she ran her index finger around the rim of her glass. As if it was a precious instrument and if he leaned closer, he might hear it sing. "Because otherwise, you did not exist."

It was as if she knew.

That was the wild notion that raced through him then, as if she had been there throughout the lonely days of his childhood once Ago was removed from his "influence." Tiziano had not taken well to the loss of his only friend and companion, sequestered away in the Tuscan countryside for years before he was sent away to a cold boarding school in darkest Britain. He had dedicated himself to finding ways, every day, to come to the attention of his tutors, his parents, Ago himself, and even, while he lived, their forbidding grandfather.

And Tiziano had not cared much if that attention was positive or negative. Not so long as it proved he existed. That he was not forgotten.

That he would not *allow* them to forget him.

For he had lived in that great house, where ghosts did not walk the halls. They were fastened to the walls in interchangeable portraits, their names known to few and important to none, every one of them a lesson in what happened to an unsung Accardi son if he allowed them to shunt him away.

It was in school that Tiziano had discovered that outrageousness could be used as leverage, and that his understanding of how to claim a room and make even those who loathed him pay attention to him was an advantage. A talent, even.

He knew perfectly well that when he'd demanded a courtesy title from Ago after his brother had been made CEO, no one expected him to do anything with it. He'd taken a great deal of pleasure in proving them all wrong.

In his own inimitable way.

Though he had not allowed himself to think of such things in longer than he cared to recall. Possibly ever.

"What of you and your sister?" he asked Annie then, too aware that she was watching him closely. When he had the strangest notion that she just might be the one person alive who could read him. When everyone else he met took him at face value.

He *wanted* them all to take him at face value, he told himself. Annie included.

But then, there was that note in his own voice he hardly recognized. A roughness there that was nothing like him. Or perhaps it was simply that he did not sound as indolent as he usually did. Too caught was he, still, in all of that solemn gray.

And all it seemed to demand of him.

He cleared his throat. "And do not tell me the two of you did not have roles to play, for surely we all do."

"It's hard to say," Annie said, with a forthrightness that stunned him. He had spent time with her now and still, he could not get used to how frank she seemed to be in all things. He kept looking for the catch. "While my parents lived, everything seemed happy-go-lucky and easy, but it is possible I only remember it that way because I lost it. It seemed less as if we played roles, Roxy and I, and more as if we were a unit. But then everything changed after the accident." She shifted against the table, but did not move any closer to him. He resented it. "My grandmother wanted to take us, but she was too old and frail by then. So we went to my aunt's and we became different people."

"How?" he asked, when he shouldn't have cared. If she had questioned him, he would have laughed and told her he didn't. But she didn't ask.

Instead, she considered the question. "Roxy acted out. And I...disappeared. Maybe we were always destined to be that way, one sister bad and the other good. Or maybe the accident is what shaped us and made us who we are now." She lifted a shoulder, then dropped it. "But either way, none of it can be changed. She gave up trying to do the right thing, but then, I gave up art. And maybe, even if my parents had lived, this is who we'd have become anyway."

"You cannot change what happened," Tiziano

agreed, again in a voice he did not recognize. "But you can always change who you are."

"Is it so easy, then?" she asked, and there was something different in her gaze. Some kind of bleak challenge that Tiziano did not wish to accept or even acknowledge. But he couldn't seem to look away. "You have the perfect opportunity before you, Tiziano. All you need to do to change, to become the man your brother wishes you to be, is marry that girl. She seems perfectly nice, by all accounts."

"How would you know?" Tiziano found himself asking. "I was under the impression she remained locked away in her convent, cursed to remain there until her father marries her off."

"She is involved with a great many charities," Annie said calmly. Too calmly. "And I think you know that. Because I know it, and everything I know about her is widely available online."

Annie regarded him for what could only have been a moment or two. There was no reason it should have felt to him like a lifetime.

Or why he couldn't tell if he was relieved or...not when she continued.

"There's no reason at all you couldn't have a lovely little life," Annie said softly. "But instead you've chosen to concoct this whole scenario with a fake mistress and an entire production behind it, just to prove that you can never, ever be anything but what you are. So tell me. Do you really think change is so easy?"

There was the sudden sound of laughter, too loud and too close. Tiziano remembered himself with a start, and straightened. As if that could change how enthralled he'd been by Annie, and every word that crossed her lips. It was a funny thing to find himself too busy *actually* being captivated by her to make sure he was *acting* as if he was.

It made him feel…outside himself, somehow.

He took a moment, looking around, but the loud burst of laughter had come from a group standing around another table nearby. It had nothing to do with him. Or with Annie.

Was he relieved or irritated? Why couldn't he tell?

Tiziano scanned the atrium, then looked back into the gallery proper. He found his brother almost immediately. Ago was engaged in what appeared to be a deep conversation with an older man Tiziano knew, even from the back, was Everard Cameron. And the virtuous Victoria herself, the fiancée he refused to claim, stood at his brother's side.

Annie was right, of course. Tiziano accepted that as he looked across the crowd at her. Victoria Cameron was wholly unobjectionable. Quite pretty, really, but then she would have to be, if her father imagined that he could sell her off in this way.

It wasn't that he was afraid of change, he told himself as he gazed at her. Because he wasn't. He never had been. It was that marrying her was the same thing as crawling into one of those gilt-edged portraits in the family gallery. It was accepting the inevitability of becoming another family ghost.

Tiziano had no interest in fading off into obscurity, whether by becoming respectable or any other means.

The Accardi family had enough ghosts as it was.

"You could say you'd seen the error of your ways tonight," Annie said from beside him, as if she knew what he was thinking when she couldn't. Of course she couldn't. For one thing, he did not think in English.

And yet Tiziano could still hear that same thing he'd seen in her gaze. He could hear that same dark current and though he could not name it to save his life, it made something inside him seem to turn over. It made his blood heat while a kind of temper beat low and hard.

It made him remember things he preferred not to recall and, worse, want things he had long since decided he could not have.

Annie wasn't finished. "You could march right over there right now," she said. "You could smile at her in that practiced way of yours and be exactly the man your brother wants you to be. You could pretend to be that man as easily as you're pretending to be with me. It's only a little bit of change, after all. It should be easy."

It seemed to take him a lifetime to angle his gaze back down to Annie. And something in him seemed to tip over, then scatter to the winds, because the gray in her gaze no longer seemed steady in the least.

All he could see in her was a storm.

And God knew there was nothing he liked better than a storm he could dance in.

He already wanted her. It was possible he'd wanted her from the moment she'd landed in a heap at his feet.

But just then, that wanting became a wildfire, and it set about burning him alive.

"I could do all of those things," he agreed, and though his voice was low, it was made of smoke and ash. He could see the way the heat got into her, too. "But between you and me, *cara mia*, I do not think my brother wants to be the man he is. So you will pardon me if I do not rush to become the man he thinks I ought to be, either."

He'd gotten too close to her as he spoke, so that their faces were nearly touching. And it was as if everything else fell away. He didn't think. He reached over and traced a pattern from her temple to her chin, as if he was sketching out all these odd and unknowable urges within him. And then, feeling intense in a way he could not have explained—as if his very life depended on it—he traced the shape of her lips, once. Then again.

And this time when he felt her shiver, he didn't pretend.

He knew exactly what it was.

The fire in him raged higher.

"You're really putting on a show," she whispered, though she didn't sound at all like herself. She did not sound calm and steady, and he took it as a victory. "It's more convincing by the day."

"Well, then," Tiziano said, his voice a low growl. "We really ought to make it good."

And he leaned in, kissing her softly, to start. Then he deepened the kiss, almost inexorably—just a taste, just a quick dip into the flames—before he pulled away.

He saw a quick glimpse of a shattered sort of expression on Annie's face, but she looked away quickly. And he had no time to follow it up, because he could feel the weight of Ago's fury from across the gallery.

And this was supposed to be a show.

So he straightened, letting his hand rest on the nape of Annie's neck, and met his brother's gaze with his own.

He did not look at his supposed intended. Because lovely as she might be, and blameless in this, it was not about her. Tiziano saw only Ago's stern expression, and did what he did best—he lifted an insouciant brow.

Daring his brother to do something about what he'd just seen.

Knowing all the while that Ago was not the sort to start a scene in public.

Tiziano told himself it was taking Ago on, instead of merely ignoring his suggestions as usual, that left him feeling so unsettled. He told himself that he was gearing up for battle, that was all.

And when he was approached by a set of high rollers who were clearly there to give Annie the once-over, he turned his smile up to its full wattage and took to his favorite stage. And a quick glance at Annie showed him she was back to her serene exterior, no hint of any *shattering* he might have imagined on her face.

But that unsettled feeling did not improve as the night wore on. When it was over, he and Annie were once again sitting together in the back of his car while London streaked by outside.

"You look unduly grim," she said, though she was looking out the window.

"I am devastated for you that you signed that non-disclosure agreement on your first day here," he murmured. "Think of the books you could sell about the truth behind the Tiziano Accardi show."

"I would never write that book." But lest he imagine she was somehow transported by sudden loyalty, she laughed. "Because it wouldn't sell. No one who's really happy and carefree spends as much time as you do *convincing* people that he's both of those things. Deep down, everyone must know it."

That landed hard. His laugh sounded hollow.

"Don't be silly," he told her. "Everyone thinks only of themselves. They take everyone else at face value."

He felt her gaze on him then, as if the gray of it was a touch. "Do they? Or do you?"

His mood did not improve when he walked her to the door of his house in Hampstead, an investment property he had never lived in and now never would, as it would always remind him of this woman and absurdly chivalrous urges like this one, to see her to the door. Tonight all of the house's modern lines seemed to gleam with particular malice against the deep December dark.

Her voice seemed to taunt him. *Does it? Or do you?*

Tiziano found himself standing there like a fool-hardy suitor as the cold and damp pressed in against them. As Annie, his mistress in name only, gazed up at him as if this was the end of a date.

As if he was a man who *dated*.

"You don't have to look at me like that," she told him, as the night seemed to spin off into mist and wonder around them. And Tiziano thought he could hear the same sort of turbulence in her voice as he felt inside. He thought he could see the echo of it in her gaze. Or maybe it was that he only wished he did. He *wished*. "No one's watching."

And it was the challenge in her voice that called to him.

Or that was what he told himself, anyway, as he moved in close. He framed her face with his hands and took her mouth with his.

Not a show this time. Not an experiment.

This was a claiming. A wish made real.

Tiziano kissed her the way he wanted to, because he had to kiss her or die, and he chose not to analyze that certainty within him. He kissed her because he couldn't bear not kissing her. Because he wanted the taste of her in his mouth again.

Always.

He kissed her again and again, flinging them both into that wildfire that raged in him, the sheer madness of the things she stirred up in him, and the wanting.

The wanting that would not leave him be.

The wanting that would take him over and turn him into someone he did not recognize—

And Tiziano had learned this lesson a long time ago.

It was no good to want things. It was worse to want people. That only meant that they could all be taken away.

Better by far to want nothing.

No matter how wild the fire was, how high the flames, he knew better.

He set her back from him, but took a deep pleasure in the way her breath came then, a ragged truth she couldn't hide. And in the way her eyes went wide, slicked with sensation.

Despite himself, he took pleasure in it all.

"What...?" she swallowed, and shook her head,

and for once sounded nothing even close to *calm*. "What was that?"

"I don't know," Tiziano gritted out. "I wish I did."

And then he made himself turn and leave her there, her panting breaths making clouds against the night.

Before he couldn't.

CHAPTER SEVEN

ANNIE DID HER best to put *kissing* out of her mind.

Because concentrating on it, she was certain, would only drive her mad.

And the last thing she needed was to be...*more* unhinged where Tiziano Accardi was concerned.

The day after the night of the kissing she wasn't thinking about and the art gallery talk of who could change and who couldn't that she couldn't stop remembering, Annie swam until she was exhausted. Lap after lap, until the motion of her arms against the water made her feel real again.

Made her feel like herself again.

Because she wasn't truly Tiziano's mistress. She needed to remind herself, apparently, that it was a role, nothing more. She could have been anyone. If he hadn't happened upon her in that stairwell, he would have chosen someone else for this and he would be behaving the exact same way. She would be looking at the very same pictures in the very same magazines. There was no point getting herself wound up about all those dark glances and what they might mean.

They meant nothing. Just because she sometimes thought she could see something in them didn't mean it was there. Or that it mattered if it *was* there, somewhere. Nothing could come of it.

And meanwhile, she had a job to do. That was the price of the life she'd have any day now, debt-free and provided for, at last.

Now that it was December, Tiziano seemed to have nothing but holiday events. Every charity threw a ball. Every group he'd even smiled at one time apparently required a celebration at the end of the year, and his presence was demanded.

And at every single event, Tiziano went out of his way to appear even more besotted than he had at the art gallery. There were the longing stares. The absent toying with her hair, a bracelet she might wear, the edge of her gown. If there was dancing he would draw her out onto the floor, then ignore the steps to every dance as he held her close—as if he could not wait to hold her the very same way in a bedroom.

Very often, Ago Accardi himself stood nearby, glowering. Sometimes the mean-looking older man she knew was Everard Cameron stood with him, clearly sharing his displeasure. But even if they weren't there, the tabloids were, and all the papers overflowed with speculation and photographic evidence of Tiziano Accardi's new passion.

She really ought to have been congratulating herself at a game well played. But the longer this went on, the more there was another aspect to her masquerade that she hadn't been prepared for.

Maybe it was because a world filled with mistresses and tabloids was so far outside the scope of her regular life. Maybe she was naive. But it hadn't really crossed her mind that people she actually knew would read the tabloids she appeared in and come to the same conclusions about the show she and Tiziano were putting on. It was her fault. All she'd been able to think about was getting out from under all of that debt. That was the only consequence that had mattered to her.

"Aren't you a dark horse," her sister Roxy said, actually calling Annie directly for the first time since she'd left for Australia.

Annie, who'd taken the call in disbelief and had assumed it was an accidental dial, now found herself staring down at her mobile as if it turned into a snake in her own palm. "I don't think I'm any kind of horse, actually."

Roxy hooted with laughter. She sounded the way Roxy always sounded. Irrepressible. Merry. Offensively unaware of the wreckage she left behind her. "Here I am feeling wretched about that whole mess, and all the while you've been angling for a much bigger payday," she said. "I'll be honest, Annie. I didn't think you had it in you."

"You've been feeling wretched?" Annie asked, pinching the bridge of her nose, because it was that or melt down. "Really, Roxy? But not wretched enough to *do* anything, though. Is that what you mean?"

"I've seen the pictures," her sister replied with another laugh. Not exactly the sound of repentance. "Why don't you sell one of those great, honking necklaces you're always swanning about in? I don't think you'll have any more issues with the bank. You can pay everything off and buy a manor house or two, if it suits you."

"I am not—" Annie began, but then stopped herself.

There in the window seat of her expansive bedroom in her guest suite in the wing of a sprawling mansion overlooking Hampstead bloody Heath.

Because what was she planning to say, exactly? That she needed her sister to cough up a few quid to pay a debt that was already paid? It seemed spiteful. Not that Roxy didn't deserve a little spite, but despite her deepest martyrish feelings, Annie understood why she'd done it. Even better, now.

Because wasn't she doing what she was doing for the same reasons? Because she'd had more than Roxy, and life was easier with more.

She started to tell her sister that she wasn't the gold digger the tabloids made her out to be, but stopped that, too. Because she might not be using the feminine wiles the world thought she was, but she was still getting the same result. And for the same reasons.

Because in a week or so, this would be over. Everard Cameron would call off the agreement he'd made with Ago, Tiziano would return to his normal life, and it would all be worth it, because Annie would be free to do as she liked. Forever.

Could she really carry on blaming her sister for causing the very situation that had led to this?

Well. Maybe not forever. But today wasn't forever, was it? "I can't believe that the first time you call me after you made me quit university is to act as if we're the same. *I* haven't stolen Tiziano Accardi's credit card."

But her sister only laughed, not sounding the least bit offended. "How are we the same? I'm lucky if a bloke buys me a drink, Annie. No one's showering me in jewels."

And though she rang off after that, and didn't pick up when Annie called her back straight away, it seemed to start a kind of avalanche.

Because suddenly, Annie was aware of other people's opinions. Regular people's opinions. It felt as much like an assault as the paparazzi flashbulb gauntlets.

The world, as far as she could tell, didn't really like the idea of everybody's fantasy boyfriend actually falling for someone.

They took against it strongly, in fact.

There were the knowing glances from some of the women, in case she didn't know he had a history. And outright hateful glares from those who'd imagined they'd had a chance. Worse still were the speculative looks from the men, imagining her performing her *duties* while they stood about having genteel conversations about the weather and the monarch's health.

Ago's disapproval, when she faced it, was almost comforting in comparison, because all he seemed to see was her inappropriate station. Not what she might get up to in bed with his brother.

There was some part of her that thought she should have been delighted that the whole world believed her to be a scandalous woman of some kind. After a lifetime of being mocked for being the very opposite, she should have found it as amusing as everyone else she knew did.

Annie Meeks, *femme fatale*. Annie Meeks, *notorious mistress*. It was absurd.

But oddly enough, no one came forward to tell the world that the Annie they knew was the last woman alive anyone should imagine would end up with a man of Tiziano's appetites. The friends from up north and her year in university who got in contact with her—in ways that ran the gamut from admiring to gentle teasing, to obviously envious, and sometimes straight-up creepy—all seemed to believe it well enough.

Annie found that the longer it went on, the harder she found it. Because it wasn't just that the world thought she was scandalous now. She probably would find that amusing someday. It was more that they all thought that she was some kind of sex goddess.

So wildly, unconquerably sensual that Tiziano Accardi himself was besotted and obsessed with her.

And it seemed wildly unfair—some kind of cosmic joke—that not only had they done nothing but kiss, but she was still the same boring virgin she'd always been.

She had never thought virginity was particularly boring before. Annie had never felt it as a burden, the way she knew some did. She'd never been seized with the burning need to get rid of it and she hadn't been holding on to it as if it was sacred, either. It was what she'd told Tiziano that night in the art gallery. She'd disappeared after the accident. She lost her parents. Maybe she'd thought that she would lose her aunt, too, if she wasn't perfect, and then what would become of her and Roxy?

So she'd been perfect in the way she knew her Aunt Sharon would understand and appreciate. Perfect marks. Perfect behavior. Perfect everything, all the time, so there really wasn't any room to worry about boys or sex or the fact she was now in her twenties and still hadn't been fussed enough to set about losing her virginity. The way her friends and her sister had done when they were still teenagers.

Annie found she worried about it a lot, now.

It seemed almost twisted, somehow, that she was being crowned the queen of a kind of passion she'd never experienced. She found herself reading articles about her own so-called *white-hot* romance and wondering who that woman was. The captivating, sensual creature the whole world seemed to think was her.

They imbued her with all manner of bizarre powers. She was a natural seductress. She used her feminine wiles to entrap every man who laid eyes on her. Even though she knew from experience that she turned precisely zero heads when walking down a street, now that she'd supposedly turned Tiziano's, her supposed beauty was treated as a fact. Something objective instead of opinion that until now, no one else had ever shared.

Even the articles that were cruel set about their cruelty very specifically. They disparaged her physical attributes—by claiming she wasn't as pretty as she thought she was, which still meant she was considered pretty. Or they mocked the way she moved, claiming she slunk about, vamping it up wherever she went. When really she was just walking in shoes that were so high she had to slow down or she would trip again.

Given that she'd met Tiziano because she'd fallen off a pair of pumps that were barely an inch high, she knew better than to tempt fate.

But it was the same issue. She was as fascinated by an angry blog post about her course, common slapperish tendencies as she was by a glowing puff piece that made her sound like an angel. Because at the center of it, no matter how much she read or how many films she watched or how much information she gathered, one single truth remained.

Tiziano was an extraordinarily famous playboy.

And Annie didn't know how to play.

One night, she excused herself from another round of brotherly acrimony and made her way to the women's lounge, which was what some fancy venues liked to call their loo. This particular grand hotel ballroom had plush stalls, flattering lights, and an entire sitting area with attendants and a small salon.

When she walked in, all the women in the room stared at her and went silent.

Then began whispering.

Another brand-new experience Annie had never had before Tiziano. Because who would be interested in whispering behind their hands about *her*? She'd been a secretary, for God's sake. And not a high-powered one, like many who were often the true power behind the flashy CEOs everyone worshipped.

She wanted to turn around and leave, but she'd already walked in. And there was something in her that thought she would actually rather die than let these people see that they'd gotten to her. Surely a sex goddess such as herself wouldn't even notice situations like this.

Annie swept over to the huge bank of mirrors along one side of the room and placed the tiny, bejeweled purse she carried on the countertop like a declaration. Then she pretended to inspect herself the way she knew the rest of them were. Looking for flaws. Looking for chinks in her armor.

But as ever, Tiziano hired only the best. She

looked flawless. Tonight, in this room, she took pleasure in that.

She snapped open her bag and fished out the lip color she'd been told to reapply at will, and did so, finding the instant glossiness almost comforting. Because this all felt like an out-of-body experience anyway. And the more she used things like gloppy lip color, the more she felt like she really might be on the stage.

And that made it easier when a woman she thought she vaguely recognized slid into place beside her at the counter.

"You must share your secrets," the woman murmured. "Who would have thought Tiziano Accardi himself could ever be brought to heel? It's an impressive feat."

"She's not impressed, in case that isn't obvious," came another voice, and Annie saw that another woman had come to stand on her other side. And though she was smiling, there was nothing friendly in her gaze. "She's jealous. The most she could get out of our Tiziano was a night."

Our Tiziano. The cheek.

"But what a night it was," purred the first woman.

"Ladies," Annie replied, and it wasn't until she saw the smile on her own face that she realized that quite without meaning to, she was essentially doing an impression of Tiziano. All lazy amusement, as if she couldn't fully rouse herself to have this confrontation. "I'm perfectly aware that Tiziano has a past filled with all kinds of adventures. But as you must know, if you know him at all, where he excels is in the present."

She did not say, *And his present is me.*

But then, she didn't have to. It was clear that they took her meaning, and more, were there to snap at each other more than at her. Annie tossed her lip gloss back in her bag and left them to it—a little too aware of the way the whispers followed her as she left the lounge.

Back out in the gala proper, the band played on and Tiziano held court his usual way. For a man who was always trying to convince everyone that he did nothing, he certainly seemed to be forever surrounded by all kinds of people who sought his advice.

The more time she spent with him, the more Annie realized that everything about him was a contradiction. Peel away one layer and ten more appeared, each one different from the last. It was hard, now, to remember how she'd felt about him when she'd met him that first day. Or how she really had thought this would all be easy, because it had never occurred to her that she could possibly fall beneath his spell.

But whatever half-formed thoughts she'd had about *men like him* back then, she'd come to realize over these weeks that in truth, there were no men like him. Whatever else he was, Tiziano Accardi was decidedly singular.

The lights in the ballroom were low because all the speeches and applause were over now. It was all about dancing and drinking, and everyone seemed to agree that was best done with as little clarifying light as possible. Annie liked it. She didn't feel as on display as she usually did.

For a moment, she was just one more woman in a pretty dress swirling around a ballroom filled with the same. She wound her way through the tables that edged the dance floor, keeping her eyes toward the front, where Tiziano stood in his pack of admirers. Annie hardly noticed them, because he still shined far too brightly, even in a darkened room.

She would have thought that spending time with him would make him somehow more unattractive to her. That it would dull the impact of all that male beauty, or at the very least, render her immune.

Instead, the opposite seemed to have happened.

She could feel it happening even now, sinking into her bones, changing her even as she moved across the ballroom floor.

It was as if he pulled her to him, but he wasn't even aware that she approached.

Annie could take in the fine cut of the dark suit he wore, tailored into a kind of love letter to his perfect form. She could let her heart do as it wished at the sight of that inky dark hair, always looking as if it was about to be tousled, or had only just been. As she drew even closer, she could let herself experience the sweet shock of his eyes that looked black in the distance, yet were blue up close.

But nothing compared to the way his gaze shifted, then found Annie in the dark.

And once he found her, his gaze grew intent.

There were still several tables between them, and Annie thought that for once, in the dark here with all the shifting lights over the dance floor, there was no harm in doing nothing at all to mask her reaction. To simply letting herself feel it.

It was as if his gaze alone set her alight. As if all that blue was the sun, and she the moon, and so she glowed. Only for him.

"Pardon me," Tiziano said to his acquaintances, excusing himself from his group and coming to meet her.

And she was sure that had they been alone, he would have caught her up and set that sensual mouth of his on hers, for a start. She could sense the savagery in him, barely contained, and what was the maddest of all was that she could feel it in her, too.

She felt like a mess. Like everything she had always prided herself on had no meaning, here between them. And yet stranger still was the way everything in her thrilled to that.

As if this was the true perfection. The way all the longing turned into heat, and held them both close. If they were alone...

But they were not.

So Tiziano did not fall upon her and Annie did not fling herself into his arms, heedless of their surroundings.

Instead, he reached out and took her hand. Then he led her out to the dance floor.

And she had things to say, but none of them found their way to her lips.

There was only this, the dancing. The music, the dark room, the way he held her close, his eyes burning into hers.

It was only later, after the music stopped, that she remembered those women in the lounge. She saw them again in the crowd, with others just like them, all wearing those speculative, jealous expressions.

Because they all thought they knew exactly what she and Tiziano were leaving the hotel to do.

"People are staring at us," she told him as he helped her into her coat, lingering a little too long as he drew it closed and buttoned it up.

He smiled, though his eyes were dark.

"You're a beautiful woman," he said, almost offhandedly, though his gaze was tight and hungry on her. Then his smile widened. "And I am remarkably handsome. Ask anyone. Naturally people stare. What else can they do?"

"That's not why they're staring, Tiziano. They think they know what we're headed off to do now."

It seemed to take him much too long to step back. To shrug into his own coat, then loop his own scarf around his neck.

"Benissimo," he murmured. "That is what we want." He studied her face then, every touch of his gaze like a caress. One dark brow rose. "Is it not?"

Annie felt her lips part, but no words came forth. No sound. Something moved over Tiziano's face, some storm she dared not investigate too closely.

Because they had to run yet another gauntlet, walking with the rest of the guests of the gala as they all exited the venue. Then they were out in the London streets as fleets of gleaming cars lined up to whisk them off to their glamorous lives.

By the time she and Tiziano got into his car, it was a relief to escape all the scrutiny—so little of it friendly. His driver pulled out into traffic, so there was nothing to do but sit in the back, listening to each other breathe.

Except Annie's breath couldn't seem to settle into a reasonable rhythm.

"I assumed that parading about as your mistress would be unremarkable," she told him.

He shifted in the seat beside her. "I'm offended, *cara*. Nothing about me is *unremarkable*. I feel certain we have touched on this simple truth before."

She ignored that. "I thought I would simply be one in a crowd, able to fade into obscurity once this ended, and spend the rest of my life testing oils against acrylics with the odd watercolor period for fun. But I'm beginning to realize that there will be no obscurity. This is how people will know me, always and forever. As Tiziano Accardi's mistress that one holiday season."

Annie remembered telling him there needed to be penalties if the rules between them were broken. It hadn't occurred to her that she would be the one to pay them.

"Some would consider this the role of a lifetime," Tiziano murmured in that way of his, sounding so deeply lazy that most might think him about to lapse off into sleep. When she could hear that dark, electric current beneath that told her he was wide awake.

"You knew this would happen," she said softly. "You like to appear to throw your money around, but the real reason you were happy to discharge all my debts and give me so much money up front is because you *knew*, didn't you? It's entirely possible that these weeks will haunt me for the rest of my life."

Tiziano's voice was dark. "I do not believe in ghosts."

She turned to him then. "I didn't understand. There's no possible way I could have understood. You knew that, too. That's why you picked me."

"Part of what makes this so believable is that you are not my usual fare." He looked at her, the lights from outside the car playing over his face and making him look like something more than just a man. She thought of that great big cat again. A jaguar prowling about the ballrooms of London, always hunting—even when he seemed to be at rest. Maybe especially then. "I told you that, though perhaps your attention was on other things at the time. Even so, it seemed the gentlemanly thing to make sure that if you wished, you could live off these weeks without ever having to worry about what became of your reputation."

Annie laughed at that, though it came out far scratchier than she intended. "And what reputation do you suppose I have? University dropout and failed secretary? Oh, yes. I imagine there will be quite a scandal to worry about there." She laughed again but he only looked quizzical. "I think you're misunderstanding me. I'm not complaining. I didn't understand the whole of it, but now I do."

"Brava," he murmured then, and it was not the first time he'd reverted to Italian when he was feeling especially sarcastic.

Annie liked that she knew that about him. Just like all the other things she knew about him. She was tempted to believe that of all the women he might have had along the way, she was the only one who knew such things about him. Because she was the only woman alive, except possibly the mother he talked about so seldom, who had ever spent this much time in his presence without taking part in what was widely held to be his favorite pastime.

What she didn't like was the fact that even random women in a loo knew parts of him that she didn't. Not that she was jealous of them. Not in the least.

But it seemed deeply unfair that she should have all of the work and all of the notoriety ever after...

yet without ever tasting the sweetness that drew all these women to him in the first place.

Yes, she told herself stoutly, *what I am concerned about here is* fairness.

She turned to face him fully in the back of the car, leaning closer, because she wanted—needed—to look straight at him while she said this. While she broke the rules she'd made.

And became the woman the whole world already thought she was.

Tiziano Accardi's mistress. For real this time.

Because it was only *fair.*

"If I'm going to be whispered about like this for the rest of my life," she said quietly, watching his gaze sharpen, "then it doesn't really seem fair that I'm not getting the full package, does it?"

CHAPTER EIGHT

TIZIANO SAT THERE in stunned silence.

He searched her face, but he could see nothing there save that same steady gray gaze, fixed on his. And a certain patience, as if Annie was prepared to wait as long as it took for him to come to grips with what she'd said.

"The full package?" he managed to ask after a small eternity dragged by. "I'm afraid I do not take your meaning."

"I think you do," she replied. And he could see the laughter all over her face then, transforming her from simply a beautiful woman into Annie. His extraordinary Annie, who never seemed to lose herself in this glittering world he inhabited. When he knew full well how easy it was for that to happen. He'd watched it a thousand times. It didn't take much for wealth to alter people. But Annie's gaze was full of mischief, her face suffused with a kind of joy, and she was still entirely herself. "You might be above propositioning women for sex in stairwells, but it turns out I'm not above doing the same in the back seat of a car. I don't know what that makes me."

"Dangerous," Tiziano bit out as his heart punched at him, a sledgehammer in his chest. "What it makes you is dangerous."

She was sitting in the seat next to him, but as she spoke she pulled her knees up, curling her legs beneath the billowing skirt of her gown like it was a throw blanket.

Tiziano had been propositioned too many times to count. In a thousand different ways, but all of those proposals had something in common. The women were usually sophisticated. In on every joke. If they came at him in a cheeky fashion, they were usually already naked.

And even though, while in Annie's presence, he found it difficult to recall the face of any other woman, he was certain he had never before had a woman sit with him like this. So artlessly, so easily.

As if what she was suggesting was not the very thing that he found himself lying awake at night imagining.

It was the intimacy of it, he thought as the car pulled off the road and into the lane that led to his Hampstead house. He had spent time with Annie. He'd made a study of her. He'd danced with her and defended her. He'd even told her things he told no one.

That had to be the reason this all sat on him differently tonight when normally, offers of sex were as notable to him as a handshake.

"Are you thinking of saying no?" she asked in disbelief when the silence between them dragged on. "You must be having a laugh, Tiziano. I would need a calculator to add up all the women I know that you've been with who were at tonight's gala alone. You're the least picky man alive. How much of a hardship could it really be—"

"Annie." His voice was far darker than he meant it to be, when inside he couldn't decide if he wished to laugh, or perhaps let out the sort of deeply male victory cry he knew was frowned upon in these enlightened times. "It is extremely indelicate to pester a man for sex. You must allow me to come to my own decision." She scowled at him and he really did laugh, then. "I have no intention of denying you anything."

She looked neither shamed nor set back. Not his Annie. If anything, her gray eyes sparkled, turning them into a shade of silver that made his chest feel tight.

"Are you secretly a romantic?" she asked, a kind of wonder in her voice. "Is that the real secret heart of Tiziano Accardi after all?"

His actual heart stopped for a moment. Then kicked back in, hard.

He had no intention of answering that.

The car drew up to the front of the house, and Tiziano had no idea what he intended to do with himself. With all this mad energy winding around and around inside him. He was very much afraid he might simply…explode.

But he knew several things at once.

This was not any old run-of-the-mill proposition. And while he was not the romantic she was accusing him of being just now—because he refused to be anything of the kind, it had been beaten out of him years ago—what he wanted from her wasn't as simple as sex, either.

A surprising position to take for a man who had long considered sex his art.

Still, the fact remained. Annie was not like his other women. For one thing, she was innocent. He was not allergic to innocence, like some. But he had also not encountered much of it in his time. Tonight he understood that it was a gift, and he intended to honor that gift as best he could.

But there was one other extremely important thing about Annie. The thing that made her different from all the others, and always would.

She was his.

Something inside him seemed to fall open, then. It was a rending, a tearing apart, but he didn't resent it. He didn't even fight it.

It was as if his life divided itself in two in that moment. There was before and there was after. Before the moment he understood what this woman was to him, and then after, when there was nothing to do but live with it.

He, who had never had the slightest intention of allowing anyone that close—

But she was looking at him, with eyes turned silver and an unmistakable invitation stamped all over her lovely face.

And much as he liked to tell anyone who listened that he was as close to a god as any they were ever likely to meet, the sad truth was that even he was no more than a man.

Just a man, in the end.

He could not have resisted this moment if he tried. And the real truth was, he had no intention of trying.

He drew Annie from the car and waved his driver off. And when she started for the stairs, he caught her by the hand and pulled her back to him.

She looked at him, her head tipped back. The cold night was making her cheeks flush, but that wide smile made him feel as if he'd staggered home drunk.

But if he was drunk tonight, it had nothing to do with alcohol.

Tiziano swept her up into his arms, enjoying the way she gasped a little, then laughed, and did nothing to conceal either response from him.

And he could feel that kind of unselfconsciousness in his sex.

He carried her toward the stairs, then in through the great doors that the staff, ever watchful, opened before them.

Once inside, he carried this woman who'd been playing his mistress—and would, tonight, become his mistress in truth—toward the gleaming white stair that flirted with the glass windows as it rose before him.

And with every step he took, Tiziano relived every moment they had shared. Every look, every breath. Every touch, played perfectly in public.

Every kiss alone.

All leading here, as if this had been their destination all along.

He wondered.

The fact of the matter was, he'd seen a great many thongs in his time. Pink lace or otherwise.

But there was only one Annie.

It was possible he had always been helpless before her.

He made it to the top of the stairs, then headed for the guest suite that Catriona, in her usual efficiency, had made certain to tell him was the one they'd used for this project, as she called it.

And he might not have been in this house in a long while, not since he'd hired a cutting-edge, of-the-moment decorator and had come to marvel at the bizarre choices made in the name of fashion. But he still found his way down the hall easily enough, and carried Annie into the rooms that she'd lived in for weeks now. Long enough that they smelled like her.

"What is that scent?" he demanded as he walked, looking for her bedchamber. "Is it you?"

She looked almost dreamy as she gazed up at him, one arm slung around his neck. "There are usually flowers in this room," she told him. "They reappear every day, like magic, in full bloom even though it's nearly Christmas."

"But there's a scent you wear, specifically." His voice was gruff. But that scent was all over him, and here in these rooms it bordered on unbearable. "And you wore it before you came here."

She blinked, then her nose wrinkled in that way that meant another laugh was on its way. Sure enough, that infectious sound only she made followed a moment later.

"That's my soap," she told him, and now her eyes were dancing. "It's the only one I use. You can't get it in your fancy soap studios, or wherever it is the likes of you get such things. For this soap, with a bit of lilac scent to make a girl feel special, all you need to do is nip down to the nearest Boots."

"Boots," he repeated blankly.

"The chemists. One on every corner. Bog standard, I'm afraid." And she smiled, but her gaze was gray again. "Just like me."

"Annie," he told her, and by this time he had mercifully located the bedroom. "You are a great many things, but not one of them is bog standard."

And then he set about showing her precisely what he meant.

Though as he set her down on her feet, there at the bed, he felt a wave of an unfamiliar sensation move through him.

It took him much too long to identify it.

Was he…anxious in some way? It hardly seemed credible. He prided himself not so much on his prowess, but on the simple delight he took in uncovering his lover's needs, then meeting them. Those she knew about and those she didn't.

But Annie was different. Everything about her was different.

It was possible that he was, for the first time in his life, worried about the outcome of this particular adventure. Not that he worried about his ability to perform. Instead, he found he was deeply concerned that she had the time of her life.

Always before, he understood then, he had simply assumed that anyone who was with him would, by definition, be having the time of her life.

And yet there was a comfort, he thought as he shrugged out of his coat and tossed it to the bench at the foot of the bed, in knowing that if this woman was unsatisfied, she would tell him so. Quite directly.

"Is something funny?" she asked, watching him closely.

"It is the package that you asked for," he told her. "I want to make certain you get exactly what it is you feel you are owed."

"That would be the full mistress experience, of course," she said. She started unbuttoning her winter coat, but he moved to brush her hands away, so that he could take pleasure in unwrapping this finest gift before him. The better to enjoy it fully. "I'm sure you know what that entails."

"A man does not usually set out to seduce his own mistress," he told her.

And the way that she looked at him, her eyes more silver by the moment, made something deep within him shudder. "Maybe if men did, they would find the experience more joyful for everyone involved."

He smiled down at her as he slid the coat from her shoulders, then let it pool on the ground at their feet. "Let us find out."

And this time, when he took her mouth, it was a different kind of claiming. Because they were alone in this room. In this house. They stood within reach of a bed. No one was watching. They were not stood in the dark outside, spinning around in the aftermath of a complicated evening.

It was as if time ceased to exist. There was only them. There was only this.

The heat. The sweet, drugging heat, that spun around and around between them, the flames higher by the moment.

"It took a team to put me into this dress," she told him, smiling as she said it. "You will have to get me out of it."

"With pleasure," Tiziano said.

And that was what he did, moving behind her and indulging himself.

He laid kisses along the line of her neck, moving his way down toward her shoulder as his hands busied themselves with the fastening of the ball gown she wore, opening a space at the bodice so it could fall to her feet. When it did, he helped her step out of the circle it made.

Tiziano drew her to him, her back to his front, and once again tasted her shoulder, her neck. He moved his way up to the delicate place behind her ear, then turned her head so he could take her mouth, too.

He wasn't sure he was going to survive this.

What he was certain of was that he'd never in his life wanted anything as badly as he wanted Annie.

So he slowed down. And made himself wait.

Because it seemed to him now that he had already waited an eternity.

He spun her around again, and finally got his hands on her as he'd imagined over the course of these last weeks. He freed her breasts from the corset-like thing she'd worn tonight and tossed it aside. And then, a wicked dream come true, she stood before him wearing nothing but a scrap of lace.

Champagne colored this time, but he found he did not mind that it was not pink.

It was still all for him.

She was breathing fast, and he liked that.

"Do you have any idea how long I have wanted to taste you?" he asked. But it was a rhetorical question at best. "Ever since the moment you crawled at my feet, and I found myself measuring your hips in my mind. Just like this."

And he set his hands there, enjoying the flare of her hips. He slid them up to her narrow waist, then finally tested the weight of her round breasts in his palms.

"You are the perfect hourglass," he told her. "Across the ages, men have gone happily to war over figures like yours. And all this time I have sat idly by, pretending I hardly noticed."

For once, it seemed his Annie could find nothing to say. He started to take off his own clothes, dispensing with his jacket, tie—

But he was too impatient and she was nearly naked, so he went down on his knees before her. He gathered her to him, getting his mouth on her last. He tasted her breasts, her nipples. He teased them into tight little peaks, and then he found his way down to that breathtaking indentation at her waist before playing with her navel, as well.

And then, at last, he moved lower, and breathed in deep.

Not lilacs, or not only lilacs. There was the faint scent of the soap she liked, but far better, the sweeter scent that was all woman and only her.

Her arousal.

Tiziano shifted her so she could lean back on her mattress. Then he settled himself between her legs, using his shoulders to keep her thighs apart. He could have removed the little bit of lace she wore, but it had figured so hugely in his imaginings that he kept it there.

He looked up the length of her body, grinning

when he found her staring down at him in a kind of dark wonder.

"Hold on, *dolcezza*," he murmured. Because he already knew she was sweet. His sweetness. "This might take a while."

And Tiziano leaned forward, taking the heat of her into his mouth. He sucked on her, through the lace she wore, and felt her jolt. Then she buckled all around him.

It was not nearly enough. He pulled back, just enough so he could hook the lace to one side, and then he truly indulged himself. He licked his way into her, reveling in the scalding, sweet heat of her core, that told him she wanted him every bit as much as he wanted her.

He felt her hands move to his shoulders, then the sides of his face, before she settled on his hair. She gripped him in tight fists, and he exulted in the pull of it, the tiny hint of pain.

Then he licked his way into her, settling in to glut himself.

Fully.

As he set a rhythm, and a pace, she quivered all around him. And then slowly, as if her body was coming alive beneath his mouth, she began to lift her hips to meet each stroke.

He felt a kind of dark triumph roar through him, setting him alight.

Tiziano was so hard he ached, but the ache was part of the pleasure, so he took it all and gave it to her.

With every lick. With every scrape of his teeth against that proud center of hers. He took her up and up. He pushed her further and further. He kept going until she stiffened, tightening all around him, and then she fell apart on his tongue.

Still he kept on going, carrying her through one peak and then taking her higher. Then higher still.

And this time, when she fell apart around him, the sob she let out was his name.

Tiziano stood, gathering her up and placing her in the center the bed. She lay there, breathing heavily. Her eyelashes were a sooty sort of smudge against her cheeks, where he could see the freckles he'd ordered her attendants to never, ever cover.

Tonight he intended to taste every last one of them.

He made short work of the rest of his clothes and then, finally, he was naked, too. He crawled into bed with her, gathering her to him, and only then did he strip the lace from her body.

And instead of concerning him, the odd sort of eagerness he felt—to do this right, to make her happy—made him almost...joyful.

As if all of this was unknown.

As if they had made this up together, the two of them, and it was only and ever theirs.

As if they were sharing this new endeavor with each other.

Tiziano felt as if he was new.

He settled in beside her and found himself something like reverent, though it was layered in with all that fire that was Annie to him. His Annie. His sweetness.

And her fathomless eyes were wide, flooded with pleasure, and fixed to his.

"Are you ready, *mia dolcezza*?" he asked, his voice a rasp in the dark.

She didn't say a word. She lifted a hand, running it over his jaw to test the dark shadow of his beard there. She followed the line of one cheekbone, then the other. Only then did she trace the shape of his lips, smiling when he pulled her thumb between his teeth.

"Because none of this is necessary," he told her, suddenly desperate that they both want this, and in the same way. With this same wildfire passion. It seemed to him then that nothing had ever been more critical. "Our arrangement does not include this. We agreed."

He shifted, rolling her body even tighter into his. And suddenly he could feel her all over him, shoulders to toes, with nothing between them.

It felt as if he was naked with a woman for the first time.

"What is this?" she asked, her eyes silver and her

lips in soft curves. "Tiziano Accardi himself, worried that a woman might not want him?"

"I'm never worried about whether or not women want me," he told her, though he was a far cry from his usual charming self. He felt stripped raw. The taste of her was in his mouth, the scent of her in his nose, and he had the strangest sensation that he would not recover from this. Not in any way he would recognize. He flipped her over onto her back and stretched out above her, as if that might give him control. "But you are not *women*, Annie. You are mine. And I find it matters a great deal to me that you..."

He couldn't say it. Because the stakes were too high. When he had never thought that there were any stakes to bedroom play.

But then, this was Annie. And he was not playing.

Tonight she was his entirely, her red hair freed from its sophisticated chignon at last, here in the dark. She was open and inviting beneath him, his sex pressed just above the place he most wished to be, and she was already shifting against him, sighing a little, a rose-gold flush taking over her skin.

"Tiziano," she said, and her gray eyes were steady again. Her voice solemn. "Don't you know? I have never wanted anyone else."

With a low groan, he fused his mouth to hers. And then everything was a mad whirl as she surged up to meet his kiss and wrapped herself around him with a grace that made him think she had made for this. Made for *him*.

And then, at last, his lungs aching as if he'd run a whole marathon to reach this moment, Tiziano twisted his hips, drove inside, and claimed his Annie at last.

CHAPTER NINE

IT WAS ALREADY too much, and then he was *inside* her. And *too much* suddenly became bigger, hotter, encroaching into everything.

Taking her over from the inside out.

For a moment Annie couldn't breathe. She felt as if she was being crowded out of her own skin, as if she'd *become* her own heartbeat, for it was so loud and so jarring in places she had never felt it before.

But she only realized that her eyes were screwed shut when she felt the touch of his lips to her temple, and his dark, raspy voice in her ear.

"Open your eyes, *dolcezza mia*," he murmured.

Annie felt as if every possible alarm inside her was going off simultaneously, each one louder than the last. She couldn't catch her breath. She couldn't *think*. And that heartbeat only got louder, wilder—

So she did the only thing she could do and opened her eyes.

Tiziano was braced above her, an expression she had never seen before on his darkly gorgeous face.

He looked...more finely wrought, somehow. As if the glorious sculpting that had made him was tighter tonight. And his stormy eyes blazed a brighter blue.

Almost as if he was a different man, lodged deep inside her, than the one she'd known when they were two separate people. Two separate bodies.

Annie shuddered, and he shifted somehow, and then it was deeper, hotter... Or maybe it was that he moved and then that he kept moving. Just a little. Just enough to send sensation crashing through her, this way and then that.

Just a little. Just enough.

First it was all too much noise, and she felt battered by it, as if she was being tossed about between her overwhelming heartbeat and the intense physical sensations, the knowledge he was *inside her*, thrown one way and the next as if she might spin out into the ether without ever managing a full breath.

But slowly, surely, it changed.

She pulled in a breath, and suddenly she could pick out the different parts of all that sensation. The deep, thick, hard-steel length of him, so deep inside her. Moving slightly, causing ripples of heat and sensation as he went. A kind of ache inside her, but it wasn't pain. It started in the place they were joined, but then it radiated out from there, connecting to all the things she'd felt about him across all these weeks, as if it had all only been waiting for this to connect.

To glow.

"Are you hurt?" Tiziano asked quietly.

And she thought he sounded different—or maybe it was because she could hear his voice and feel it beneath her skin, the way she always did, but now he was part of her body as he spoke.

It was almost too much for her to bear.

"Am I meant to be hurt?" she asked, not sure if she felt…cross. Or possibly like crying. Or as if she'd somehow become a kind of sob herself and she wasn't certain if she was trapped somewhere or if she had already broken wide open.

Annie moved beneath him, restlessly, not sure if she wanted to move closer or farther away. But whatever she chose, the heat followed her.

Not only did it follow her, it grew more intense every time. So intense that part of her wanted to stop—

But not enough to actually stop.

"Haven't you heard the grim and gory tales of virginities crudely taken?" Tiziano asked, sounding so deeply indolent that it was a wonder he could hold himself above her the way he did. So epically languid that she wanted to dig her nails into his arms, that she hadn't realized she was gripping so hard. When she did, he smiled. "And depending on how medieval the story in question, bloody sheets waved before the cheering peasants and so on."

"Of course I've heard stories," she said, frowning up at him, even as her hips followed his movements. As if they knew things she didn't. "But I assumed it was because the poor women in those stories were in the hands of inexperienced lovers. Not…you."

Tiziano laughed, and Annie felt her chest seem to split wide open, because it was a real laugh. And while she'd heard it before, this was different. Because he was naked and inside her, and she knew, with a surge of some kind of wisdom she'd never touched before, that this was the real him. All Tiziano, no show.

Her heart kicked at her again, but this time in a kind of awe.

Because his eyes were always blue. But never quite like this.

Never so intense that she felt as if she was the same storm in him.

"I am delighted to live up to your expectations of me, *dolcezza*," he said then, and his voice was still so low. Still so raspy. And yet he sounded something like hushed, as if these were vows. As if this was a ceremony, here in the fire they'd built between them. "It will be an honor."

And then, as if he had all the time in the world, Tiziano bent down and began to press kisses to her face. All over her face, but never quite finding her lips.

When she made a sound of complaint, he only laughed again. And it was darker this time. He switched his attention to her neck, her collarbone, each kiss more maddeningly decorous than the last when he was still huge and hard within her.

Annie pushed at him, outraged, though she couldn't have said what she wanted. What she did feel certain of was that he knew. He *knew* and yet he was playing games with her. And she had never been more sure of anything in her whole life than the fact that this was no *game*. It was too important. It was life-altering and he was *languid*—

But Tiziano pulled her over with him then, so that she sprawled on top of him, and that was new. And when she moved, she felt him inside her in a variety of new and concerning and marvelous ways.

"Sit up," he told her.

He helped her rise, and then watched her through narrow, proud eyes as she tested the new fit. She liked it.

Annie pulled her lower lip between her teeth and then slowly, carefully, began rocking herself against him.

And maybe she got carried away that way. Maybe she lost herself a little. She rocked and she rocked, chasing the wonder of it. The slick fit. The crash of light and longing inside her every time she dragged herself against him.

At some point, his hands moved from her hips and started to do magical things to her breasts, her nipples. And then, when she thought it could not possibly get any better, Tiziano reached down to the place they were joined and pressed, hard.

And this time, when she spun apart, Annie heard his laughter all around her. And it helped her find her way home through all those spinning, dancing stars that swept her away for a while.

She was panting, she felt bright red everywhere, and she didn't know they'd moved. It was a surprise, then, to find that she was on her back again and he was between her legs, pulling her knees up and wide so he could settle comfortably between her thighs.

Impossibly, she felt all that fire inside her burn brighter. Hotter.

When she would have said it had clearly burned itself out.

He said something in Italian, a dark, lyrical thread that seemed to wrap itself around her, and yet she could feel the way he held himself back. She could sense it, somehow, in the way he looked at her.

And she didn't want that from him. Not here. Not now.

"There's only so much generosity a woman can take, Tiziano," she whispered, and she hardly recognized her own voice. But then, she hardly cared. "Please, I beg of you, be selfish."

"I live to serve," he said then, his eyes glittering and a certain kind of gravel in his voice.

And Annie thought that by now, she knew. She understood what was between them. All the many contours of this fire. Hadn't he thrown her into the heart of it tonight? Too many times to count?

But as Tiziano moved over her at last, sweeping her off into a dark glory she could not begin to comprehend or explain, she understood that while she'd understood he was holding back, she hadn't understood what that meant.

Because this was the storm.

This was him.

At last.

It was a wildfire run amok. It was wave after wave, a tsunami of sensation. It was thunder forever, endless flashes of lightning, and she lost track of how many times he threw her off into the electric glory of it, burning her alive.

Yet each time, he brought her back.

Because every time, there was more.

Until, at last, he found a fire so hot that even he burned up.

And finally, as Annie tipped off into ash once more, Tiziano came with her.

She thought maybe she'd died. She wasn't certain that she hadn't. She had no idea how long it was, there in the dark. The two of them together, half stars, half fire, and not quite themselves again.

He had moved his weight off her, but lay beside her, his heavy arm anchoring her to the bed. And there were too many new things to parse, so Annie didn't try. She concentrated on the weight of his arm, all that smooth muscle, holding her here. Reminding her she was still a part of the earth. She lost herself a while in the scent of his skin, something that reminded her of the seaside, a windswept salt. Or the faint near-abrasions she could feel on her skin that made her prickle all over in a dark delight, because she knew they came from the scrape of his beard.

It felt like an intimacy almost too much to bear.

Annie lay there in the dark, slowly learning how to breathe again, and she didn't know if Tiziano was asleep or awake. But it hardly mattered. There was light outside the great glass windows and she turned her head toward it, pleased to feel the moon all over her tonight, like a kind of holiday blessing.

And after all these parties, balls and gowns and gatherings of every type, this was the first time she found that she felt the slightest bit of Christmas spirit at all.

A little bit of moonlight, and her very first lover, was all it took.

Her breath left her then, hard. And Annie had a sudden, stabbing moment of clarity so intense that she thought it might have knocked her off the bed if she hadn't been lying down. If his arm wasn't holding her tight, keeping her near.

Tiziano was her first lover, yes. But she would not take another. Despite the fact that she had made herself notorious in some circles as this man's mistress, a role she now inhabited in full, this was not a lifestyle. Mistresses moved from one man to another, she knew. It was why the men at these parties looked at her the way they did, as if inspecting merchandise.

But she would be a mistress to one man only.

If anyone other than Tiziano had come up those stairs that day, she would have been unmoved. She would have gathered up her documents and gone about her day. Even now she would be lying in her bedsit, glaring stonily at her ceiling. Concentrating not on the moonlight, but on the sounds of her busy neighborhood outside and the debt she couldn't pay.

Tiziano was the only man alive who could have tempted her away from her life. Not because she'd liked her life so much, but because only this man could have convinced her to agree to behave in a way that was fully alien to all she'd ever thought she was before.

More than that, she liked it.

Oh, my God, she thought to herself, lying naked beside him. *I'm in love with him.*

He murmured something in Italian beside her, and pressed his mouth to her shoulder. She shivered, just a little, the flames licking at her once more. But when he did not move again, Annie released the breath she'd been holding and turned back to the moonlight.

But she didn't feel like Christmas this time.

Instead, she felt a surge of grief. Not because she was in love with him, but because she wished—with an intensity that she would have said she'd healed from long ago—that her mother was still alive. That her grandmother was still here. That her aunt had been a warmer guardian. That her sister was less… herself.

Because she would have given anything to have someone to talk to, just now.

She would have given everything she had to have

someone to tell that she felt these things. To be able to say it out loud. To sit with someone who already loved her and try to imagine that she would survive this. Him.

Of all of them, it was her wise, warm grandmother she would have killed to see just now. She wished she could sneak from this bed and go find her nan in her sweet little cottage in the Cotswolds. She had always been delighted to hear from her girls. She had never been impatient, or disinterested, or anything but engaged when they'd told her stories about their lives.

The cure for broken heart, she had always said, *isn't wallowing, though of course you must wallow first. With cake, in my opinion. But the true cure is time. And the best way to honor the passing of that time is to grow things.*

She would take Annie out into the garden, in those years when Roxy refused to visit. And that thickly overgrown garden was the only place she'd ever felt safe enough to express how low she felt. How much she'd missed her parents and how little she felt she could show that in Aunt Sharon's house. Because she knew that she and Roxy were her aunt's act of charity. Not love.

Her nan never told her she was wrong for feeling as she did. Together, they would get their hands in the dirt. They would talk about seeds and water, rain and sun. When Annie would come next, seeds she'd planted would be in bloom. And later in the summers, there was fresh veg to eat.

And her grandmother was right, always. There was no cure for grief. But the tomatoes were plump and juicy. The flowers were bright and happy. The roses smelled sweet and the wisteria could never be contained to its trellis. And somehow, the water and the sun, the earth between her fingers and the wind in her face, helped her heal.

Beside her, Tiziano stirred.

Annie thought of seeds in the earth. Grief and love, mirror images of each other. She turned toward him, smiling even though she felt that huge sob inside her again. Because this time it felt far more unwieldy.

His eyes were closed and so, for a moment, there was nothing to do but behold the singular beauty he wore too easily. Those dark lashes that were entirely too long for a man. His sculpted face in repose, nearly angelic, when he was anything but.

Then his eyes opened, for once not the least bit sleepy, and he pinned her with all of that impossible blue.

"You've never had a mistress before, have you?" Annie asked.

She had no earthly idea why she'd led with that. She hadn't even known the words were on her tongue. She blinked, not sure she if was appalled with herself or was secretly pleased.

And in any case, Tiziano only laughed.

"There are established responses in moments like these, *cara mia*," he said, as if he was chiding her, but she could hear the laughter laced in his voice. "I will compliment you, you will compliment me, and we will both note—perhaps at the same time, how clever—that we are yet naked. So many possibilities might present themselves. I might carry you into the bath, where even greater pleasures await. I might make better use of this bed." He shook his head, his gaze warm and blue, all over her like the moon. "But no. Not my Annie. It must always be an interrogation."

She wanted to apologize, but settled for a smile instead. "No one's around to watch us here," she said, reasonably enough. "It seemed as good an opportunity as any to ask you the real questions."

"The real questions that most wish to ask me involve my bank account." Tiziano's eyes lit with that dark amusement she found she craved. "The content of my wallet. The art on my walls and whether it has been recently appraised. The exact number of sports cars I have at my disposal. Whether or not my brother seeks a woman to provide him with the Accardi heirs everyone knows must someday appear. Normal questions." He moved to prop himself up on one elbow, letting his other hand move where it would over her body. He seemed to find the curve of her hip most entrancing. "Are you certain you wish to know the history of my mistresses at such time? I feel that can only lead to tears and dismay."

"I think you've been putting on a show," Annie said quietly. And since he was moving his hands where she liked, she did the same—finally indulging herself. There were those pectoral muscles of his that were so fascinating, and even more so because, when not hidden away beneath his shirt, they were dusted with dark hair. Something she would have said, in the abstract, she didn't find attractive. And yet when she touched him it made her shake, deep inside. And it made that ache between her legs intensify. "And you don't like anyone backstage. So no mistresses. Not like me. I reckon I'm the only one."

His gaze was still a gleaming thing, but it was no longer amusement she saw there. There was something much darker. Still, his voice remained light. "The first and the last," he agreed, but not in his usual careless tone. She clung to that. "Does this please you?"

"Well, yes." And Annie smiled at him, not caring the way she should that he might see things in her yes, all over her face, that were better hidden. "I was worried there was a standard I needed to live up to. But I am the standard."

That wariness in his gaze eased. "Indeed you are."

Annie followed the urge inside her and pressed her mouth to that hollow between his pectorals, then followed the spear of dark hair down over his ridged abdomen, tasting him, inhaling him, imprinting on him.

And when she reached those fine V-shaped furrows that seemed to guide her directly where she wanted to go, she paused and looked up at him. He

was on his back now, one arm behind his head looking down at her with an indulgent sort of heat that
made everything inside her seem to catch on fire.

"Just wait," she told him quietly. "Now that I have
all the tools at my disposal, I'm going to be the best
mistress that ever was."

"Is it a competition?" he asked.

As if he felt it, too, this impossible need. This
same longing she felt inside.

But she knew him well enough to know that he
would never admit these things. Maybe he couldn't.

"It could never be a real competition," she said,
striving for a lightness she did not feel. "We are set
to end this the moment your potential arranged marriage is taken off the table."

And it was only once the words were out, hanging
there between them, that she admitted to herself that
what she wanted was for him to argue the point. To
tell her he needed more. That he needed *her*.

That this night had changed everything for him,
too.

His eyes seemed a particularly dark shade of blue
as he gazed at her, though his mouth did not curve.
"What cannot last is all the sweeter for the swiftness
of its passing, I think. *È così*."

She didn't believe he truly felt that way. But she
also didn't want to argue the point. Not now. Not
when she was so raw, and this was so new, and everything was different whether he wanted to admit
it or not.

And so Annie did not speak to him of love. Or grief. Or the state of her heart. She did not tell him what she had to lose here, or share with him her deep certainty that for every bit of pleasure he brought her—and she had never known such pleasure existed—he would be sure to bring her pain, too.

She planted all of those things inside her, deep, and knew that they would grow. In their own time. In their own way.

Annie held Tiziano's gaze, and she angled herself over the hardest part of him, already bold and ready for her again. Long and thick and so inviting it made her mouth water.

"You tell me if this is a competition," she suggested. "You are the one with experience."

There was that hard glittering thing in his gaze, then. She felt it echo deep within her own body. "It can be whatever you wish it to be, *dolcezza mia*."

Annie moved lower, because all the ways that he was male where she was female fascinated her. And what a strange sort of fascination this was, that it wasn't something to think about. She didn't want to analyze this. She wanted nothing more than to explore him.

Preferably with her mouth.

"Let's see how it goes," she told him. "Because between you and me, I think I'm going to win."

"I have no doubt," he said, his voice little more than a growl.

And when she felt his hands in her hair, she bent down and set about exploring him. Learning him. Inch by glorious inch.

CHAPTER TEN

CHRISTMAS EVE CAME too soon, Annie thought.

She stood in the ballroom of one of London's most exclusive hotels surrounded on all sides by a variety of decked halls, brightly decorated Christmas trees, and the usual crème de la crème of British society, dressed in sumptuous jewel tones and happy metallics. She didn't know which charity ball this was. They all ran together. Annie only knew that she was looking forward to Christmas. She needed the quiet. She needed a bit of the expected peace on earth, so she could see if there was any peace to be found inside her.

Because she was ready for a little break from being Tiziano Accardi's mistress. Even if thinking such a thing made her whole body ache, as if she'd already lost him. Not that she *wanted* to lose him, but this much intensity, day and night, when she already knew how it would end...

It was a lot, that was all. Annie needed to regroup.

And besides, tonight was supposed to be the night

Tiziano's engagement to Victoria Cameron was announced. Despite his very public affair with Annie that the tabloids had talked about exhaustively for the past six weeks, the engagement plans had not been called off.

The last she'd heard, his brother was still determined that the match should take place.

Tiziano had informed her almost offhandedly the other day that if the announcement was made, nothing would change. They would carry on as they had all along, though it was a certainty that the tenor of their tabloid coverage would change.

But you were so sure this would work, she had said, not sure if she was upset for him that it hadn't— or pleased that she was getting more time with him than the original two weeks he'd promised. *It must be upsetting that this is not going according to plan.*

It is fine, he had said, though he neither looked nor sounded like it was fine. *The tabloids will focus on my wickedness, not yours. That might be the push Everard Cameron needs to do what he should have done weeks ago.*

But as he said it, he toyed with her fingers in his, and the look on his face was not the one he'd worn in that long-ago stairwell. It was too…intense.

Annie tried to tell herself that made it all better when the truth was, she loved him too much, too hard. And there was no possibility that she would not feel what was done to him even more keenly than anything that might be said or done to her.

That he didn't understand that, or feel the same, was its own ache.

The past couple of weeks had been a kind of waking dream. On the one hand, nothing had changed. Outwardly. Annie lived the life of a kept woman because that was what she was—in every respect, now. She swam her laps, she let her attendants turn her into a nightly swan, the same as ever. And then she and Tiziano would go out to yet another function to convince even more people that theirs was a scorching love affair with no equal.

But the difference was, when they left their engagements at the end of the night, he didn't drop her home with a few growled words and the odd kiss.

Sometimes he couldn't bear to wait out the drive and so he took her there in the back seat of the car, surging into her as London rolled by outside the windows while she muffled her sobs of joy in the crook of his neck. Sometimes when she was dropped off at his flat before an event, he threw her over his shoulder, and carried her to his bed there, a pageant in itself, where he would undo all the hard work her attendants had done and laugh while he did it.

Sometimes everything was too intense, too wild. It felt as if they'd opened a kind of Pandora's box of need and hunger, and Annie was very much afraid that there would never be any return to something like normal. That she would never, ever be herself again.

Other times, she didn't care if she was normal

again, whatever that was. At night, they would sleep tangled up together in some bed or another, in these places he owned but did not truly inhabit, and she would try to caution herself. Every spring turned into fall, she knew that. And there was no escaping the winter that would follow.

She told herself these things again and again.

But it was hard to remember what she knew when Tiziano smiled at her. When he called her all manner of florid Italian endearments in public, for show, but only ever called her *dolcezza* in private.

Dolcezza mia. My sweetness.

Annie had never felt particularly sweet. But for him, she was. For him, she felt like a confection. A dessert of a woman instead of the meat and two veg, stolid and unflashy sort she'd been before she'd met him.

If she was sweet, he made her that way.

After that first night they'd finally come together, she'd stopped looking for other people's reactions. Maybe she didn't want to know if they could see how things had changed, stamped all over her face. Annie felt too raw. More, she was afraid she was a kind of walking billboard of love and sex and a heart already half-broken, because this was never meant to last.

But as the days passed, that eased.

Because it was impossible to love Tiziano without surrendering entirely to the moment, each moment, she had with him.

Annie stopped trying.

I don't want to get ahead of myself, Roxy had said in one of her calls. She'd started ringing almost daily now, though neither one of them commented on it. *But you do seem to have...lightened up a bit lately.*

I'm a very famous mistress now, Annie had told her grandly, because she knew her sister was perhaps the only one who would laugh at that—in the spirit intended, that was. *And do you know what mistresses do all day?*

Everyone knows what mistresses do all day, Roxy had replied dryly. *Much as all the riches and jewels and fancy parties seem appealing, the sex on tap does sound a bit like work, to be honest.*

Annie had been going to talk about all her spa visits and general loafing about, but had sighed instead. *Some people are allergic to work, I know.*

But her sister was unrepentant, as ever. *I think I'm more interested in being a bit of a spoiled wife,* she'd said, as if she could choose such a thing from a menu. *All the fun and games of the mistress life, but you're allowed to have a headache. And all you have to do is pop out a kid, and there you go. Lifestyle assured forever.*

Merry Christmas, Roxy, Annie had said, and she'd even laughed. When she knew that if her sister was in Britain, she would have felt honor bound to go and wring her neck. Something about the distance made it all right to talk like this, as silly as if they were still young. Or it made it better, anyway.

And how could she complain, really, when Roxy's betrayal had led straight to Tiziano?

Because even though Annie knew that she was on a speeding, out-of-control train that had no possible chance of doing anything at all but crashing, she couldn't regret him.

Not one moment of him.

One of these summers I'll have to come back, Roxy had said yesterday. *We can go to Whitby the way we did with Mum and Dad. Eat wretched, soggy sandwiches by the sea and complain about the cold.* She'd seemed to remember herself then. *If you're not, you know, traipsing in and out of various castles or whatever it is rich people do.*

There were so many things Annie could have said to that. She could have demanded a kind of reckoning. She could have reminded her sister that they still needed to have a frank word about debts and responsibilities and all the rest.

But she found herself thinking instead of swimming by the sea. Of dancing around and around in a caravan, with all that helpless, reckless laughter, because they'd no idea what was to come.

Because no one ever knew what was to come.

If they'd known, if they'd had the slightest idea, they would never have done those things in the first place. They would have wrapped themselves up in cotton wool and locked themselves away.

I'd like that, she said softly. *But I'll be hiding my wallet.*

That's fair enough, Roxy had replied. *As long as your flash bloke doesn't, it'll be all right.*

Annie would have said that her relationship with her sister could never be repaired. But each time she put down the phone these days, she felt better. Lighter.

As if she'd gone ahead and forgiven Roxy when she hadn't been paying attention.

Maybe it made sense, she thought now, as Christmas was nearly upon her and this was the season for that sort of thing, wasn't it?

Meanwhile, she and Tiziano were still playing their same game. Because his brother showed no signs of backing down. And even though Tiziano had been certain that the father of his supposed intended would sort this out long since, the man hadn't yet done it.

Remember when you thought this would take a week, maybe two? she'd asked in the car over tonight.

Tiziano's hand had been on her leg, his thumb moving in that restless manner that let her know that he was not satisfied by the way they'd made each other groan at the house before they'd left for the Christmas Eve ball. *I'm devastated that you no longer enjoy my company,* dolcezza.

He looked more handsome tonight than he ever had, but then, that was true every night. The more time Annie spent with him, the deeper into that she got, the more beautiful he became.

It was unfair. But then, it all felt unfair these days.

I don't want this to carry on past your engage-

ment announcement, she'd said. Though every word felt like a knife between her ribs. *That's to be tonight, isn't it?*

There will be no announcement, he'd growled at her.

Because it's all fun and games to play at being a mistress, she'd continued softly. *But not if there's an actual wife waiting in the wings.*

She'd come to that decision in the pool. And she'd contained the sobs that had surged up in her to beneath the smooth surface of the water. And until she'd said it out loud, she hadn't been sure she would say it at all.

There will be no announcement, Annie, Tiziano had said again, darker still.

And then he'd spent the rest of their ride to the grand hotel giving her a great many other things to think about.

It was one of his talents.

Now Annie stood in a fairy tale, just like a princess, but she wasn't one. The mistress didn't get to swan off into the sunset with Prince Charming. Everyone knew that.

While Tiziano was off having his usual tense word with his brother, Annie did what she always did at these functions. She kept to herself, smiling mysteriously, and doing her best to look as if she was perfectly at her ease. The usual people were busy whispering the usual things all around, but now that she really was the woman they'd imagined her to be all this time, Annie found she was far less interested in the things they might have to say about her.

Because it didn't matter what happened. They didn't know him.

Annie was the only one who did.

Though she sometimes wished she didn't, because one of the things she knew about Tiziano was that he would always be more committed to the show than to her. Than anything else at all. Because he thought the show was all he had.

And she knew better than to try to convince another person that she could make up for the things they lacked. Look at her sister. She'd imagined she could take the place of their parents for her sister—but she hadn't. Roxy had mourned them all the same, and turned that mourning into all kinds of bad decisions. Annie's credit rating being only one of them.

She finished off the last of the one glass of wine she allowed herself—because it was best to keep her wits about her, here in this lion's den—then turned to place it on the nearest table. And when she straightened, she found another woman standing before her.

But not just any other woman.

It was Victoria Cameron. The saintly woman that Tiziano's brother had every intention of announcing as Tiziano's fiancée by the end of the night.

For a moment they gazed at each other, and Annie braced herself. Even as she told herself that there was no need, surely. Tiziano had the right to be with anyone he wished.

But she was still ready for a slap.

Instead, Victoria smiled. "I thought we should meet."

"Whatever for?" Annie found herself asking, idly enough that she could almost have been doing a Tiziano impression. "Surely it gives everyone far more to gossip about if we stand on different sides of the ballroom, glaring daggers at each other."

Victoria was a willowy, effortless blonde, a monument to poise and good breeding in a golden dress. Everything Annie was not—and yet somehow, Annie didn't feel diminished standing next to her. Maybe it was because Victoria's smile looked real. And she didn't seem aloof and snobbish like so many of the others Annie had encountered in ballrooms just like this one.

Not to mention the bathrooms.

"They'll do that anyway," Victoria said with a shrug. "Whether they have ammunition or not. Between you and me, I think that's all they know how to do."

"I wouldn't know." Annie took a chance and grinned. "Haven't you heard? I'm common as muck."

Victoria laughed. And then, to Annie's great surprise, leaned in and linked her arm with Annie's.

"My father is the one who wants me to marry Tiziano," she confided. "And I've been all for it, because the only thing I want in this life is to escape my father. It sounded like fun, to be honest. He's famously unserious and so I thought everything would be fizzy and funny, and then he'd go off somewhere and leave me on my own. Bliss in an arranged package, to my mind."

Annie felt as if her chest was in a tight fist. It was hard to get a breath.

"He's not unserious at all, actually," she managed to get out.

It seemed such a foolish thing to say. Especially when Victoria looked at her with a wealth of compassion in her gaze and she understood that somehow, she'd given herself away to *this woman*, of all people.

"I've seen the way he looks at you," Victoria said softly. "I would have said he didn't have it in him. I don't like that he does, because what I want is something shallow. Easy. A business arrangement, nothing more."

Annie felt a sudden, strange responsibility for this woman, which didn't make any sense. She was a stranger. A stranger who might marry the man she loved, no less.

"You should marry because you love someone," she said, frowning at the Cameron heiress, who could not possibly have known a moment's struggle. "And for no other reason."

Victoria smiled at her then, but there was something sad in her gaze. "I'll leave the love to you, I think. I'm afraid that for some of us, that will never be in the cards. Don't worry," she continued when Annie started to argue that. "I'll tell Ago Accardi myself. He and my father like to make decisions between themselves, but the good news is, Ago is the gentleman my father is not. *He* won't force me to marry his brother if I don't want to. And I don't. That's what I wanted you to know."

Annie wanted to tell her it wasn't necessary. That she might as well go ahead and marry Tiziano, because the kind of surface-only relationship Victoria was talking about was exactly what he wanted. It was the only thing he knew. It was the kind of show he liked best. This deeper, soul-shifting nonsense couldn't last, no matter how sweet he thought it was for now.

And she doubted very much he would allow it to happen with anyone else.

Besides, she needed to get some space from all of this. The character she was supposed to be, according to the tabloids. The mistress, the jumped-up secretary. Tiziano himself. She needed to catch her breath, at the very least. An engagement announcement would be the perfect opportunity to bow out of this whole mad circus.

Annie opened her mouth to tell Victoria all of this, but instead, all that came out was a soft "Thank you."

And then she stood there, trying to reconcile that response with the swirling ache inside her, as Victoria nodded, squeezed her arm once more as if they were friends, and then walked away.

She was still standing there, unsettled, when Tiziano came to find her.

"Dance with me," he commanded her, his mouth

at her ear. She had to fight to keep her eyes from falling shut. She had to fight to keep from leaning into him. "It's nearly midnight and there's still no announcement. Ago blustered about, as he does, but I think we might well be in the clear."

Annie could have told him there would be no announcement. She didn't know why she didn't. Instead, she let him draw her out onto the dance floor. And then she let herself ache as they swayed together, as he gazed down into her eyes. Then, eventually, she had to close her eyes and rest her cheek against his shoulder, because she did not wish him to see the way that ache grew and grew inside her.

Because Tiziano loved nothing more than his show.

And later, even as he moved inside her with that fierce, possessive look on his face, pinning her to the bed with his masterful strokes, she knew that no matter what he felt, he never would.

Tomorrow, or soon after, his brother would tell him that he'd received the reprieve he wanted.

Tiziano would tell her that his plan had worked.

And soon enough, this arrangement would end.

Maybe not immediately. But what good would it do to draw it out?

Sooner or later, Tiziano would remember that sharing himself led nowhere he wished to go.

Sooner or later, he would end it.

There was no avoiding her broken heart. Even the woman who wanted to marry Tiziano could see how in love Annie was. She probably also saw how doomed that love was, though she had been too polite to mention it.

The only thing Annie could do was choose the *when* of it.

And so, much later that night, when it was already turned Christmas, she crept out of that sprawling house in Hampstead. She took only a few of the things she'd brought with her, and a very few of the things that had been provided for her. She wrapped herself up against the cold and then headed for the village, though it was a long way to walk at that hour and the night smelled like snow. She found a cab discharging merrymakers and offered the driver an astonishing amount of money to drive her out of London.

Because the seeds she'd planted inside her had started to bloom into despair, and there was only one place in the world she could think of to go and nurse them.

Just until they could be flowers again. And she would be close enough to whole by then, she hoped, so she could appreciate them for what they were. Just what they were.

What they had always been despite her foolish heart.

Just what they were, and nothing more.

CHAPTER ELEVEN

WHEN TIZIANO WOKE to find the bed empty, he didn't like it, but he didn't think much of it. He stretched in the early morning light, congratulating himself on having worked things out so well.

For Christmas Eve had come and gone, and Ago had made no announcements. Everard Cameron had made no claims. Despite all the pressure of these past weeks, Tiziano's engagement had not been announced—whether he liked it or not—to all of those people crowded into the ballroom last night.

He'd won.

His brother might not have admitted it yet, but Tiziano knew the truth. He had won the battle. This engagement was not going to happen.

More importantly, Ago had made a threat and been unable to carry through with it.

This meant two things. One, that his brother was going to think twice before he tried to come for Tiziano again.

And two, that Tiziano was perfectly free to indulge himself completely without having to worry about rumors, tabloid coverage, or the grind of so many formal events.

He prowled into the expansive bathroom suite, expecting to find Annie curled up in the tub. Or perhaps in the adjoining room, tending to her reflection in a way he'd never seen her do, but assumed all women must. Or perhaps selecting items from her wardrobe.

But she was nowhere to be found. Not in the guest suite that had been allocated to her. And not, he ascertained after an irritated tour through this absurd mausoleum of a house, anywhere else.

It was only then that he inquired about her whereabouts, only to discover from his staff that she'd left sometime before dawn.

He was on the phone to Catriona within seconds, because he had to do something. Because Annie couldn't leave him. How could she have *left* him?

The way that his heart thumped at him might have knocked him over if he hadn't taken some kind of action.

"Give me her London address," he barked down the line.

"There's no need," Catriona replied smoothly. "We broke her lease when she moved into your Hampstead property. The assumption being that once the project is at an end, she would have the means to ensure that wherever she lived next, it need not be a bedsit of such questionable quality."

"Where would she go?" Tiziano gritted out. He could remember every last thing Annie had said to him, and tried to go through it all, looking for clues. "She was raised by an aunt, was she not?"

"She was," came the crisp reply, and so quickly that Tiziano knew Catriona was not consulting any notes. She'd committed all of this to memory, because she was a gem without price. "But I believe her aunt's Christmas traditions center upon Spanish beaches. Even if Miss Meeks did intend to meet up with her, it's unlikely she could manage to get on a commercial flight this early on Christmas morning."

That was when Tiziano realized that it was, in fact, Christmas morning.

He'd known that, clearly. Because he'd known last night was Christmas Eve. But somehow, that hadn't given him so much as a moment's pause when he'd pulled out his mobile to phone Catriona.

Something he knew wouldn't have occurred to him at all if he hadn't spent these last weeks in the company of a secretary. Who had always been quite vocal about his privileged behavior when it came to his staff.

"I apologize," he said now, though the words felt strange in his mouth. And if he wasn't mistaken, shocked Catriona as much as they did him. "I'm not myself. You should not have to field unhinged calls for me on Christmas morning."

There was a short pause. And then, his unflappable assistant coughed, as if she was as uncharacteristically taken aback by this moment as he was. "It's no bother," she said after a moment. "The grandchildren aren't due for another hour."

Tiziano then had the distinct impression that they both stood there, in their respective homes, contemplating the fact that while Catriona knew every single detail of Tiziano's life, this was the first he had ever heard of any grandchildren. And, by extrapolation, that she was a mother. Possibly a wife in possession of a partner. And presumably had an entire rich life of her own.

Perhaps it is not so surprising that Annie left you, he told himself acidly.

"And speaking of grandchildren," Catriona said, in a tone that made it clear she did not intend to speak about her own, possibly ever again, "Miss Meeks and her sister were the only beneficiaries of their grandmother's will." She cleared her throat, which was as good as another woman's entire emotional breakdown, and then it was done. "If I had to wager, I would guess that if she went anywhere it would be to her grandmother's cottage in the Cotswolds. I will text you the address at once."

"Thank you, Catriona," Tiziano said, with excessive formality. He paused. "And I hope you have a very happy Christmas."

Catriona made a strangled sort of noise, then rang off.

Tiziano stayed where he was, in the oppressively over-white foyer of this house. He was concerned about the state of his heart. Because the house around him felt like a hospital already, and because his heart was making all kinds of noise. Every beat of it seemed to hurt, as if something was terribly wrong with him. As if he was cracking apart—

But there was no time to worry about such things, he told himself darkly. He had to find Annie.

In short order, Tiziano threw on some clothes and drove out of North London grateful that not all of his cars were fanciful, low-slung, sporty affairs. Because as he headed into Gloucestershire, the weather got worse, matching his mood by the mile, and he was grateful that he was in a Range Rover instead of an Aston Martin.

By the time he reached the village he was after, according to his navigation software, the world had become a proper Christmas card.

He drove down winding lanes piled high with snow. There were thatched roofs piled with snow and curls of smoke in the wintry air. There were candles in windows, twinkling lights on trees, and Tiziano was so agitated by the Christmas of it all that he felt like some kind of ravaging beast by the time he found the place he was looking for. A tiny little thatched cottage at the very end of an untouched lane.

It looked cozy and inviting, with hints of lights in the windows, and he resented it. Deeply.

At least she was warm. Even if she would have been far warmer if she'd stayed where she belonged, right next to him in bed.

Tiziano's temper was black and darkening by the moment as he threw himself out the Range Rover and stomped through the snow toward the front door, such as it was. It had clearly been fashioned for people a tenth of his size. He felt as if he was in some kind of fairy tale—and had been cast in the role of the hulking villain, a seething black roar across all of this pristine whiteness.

A feeling that only intensified when the door opened a crack. Then wider, to reveal Annie standing there.

Frowning up at him as if he was a stranger.

"What are you doing here?" she asked, as if that was not obvious.

"At the moment, *dolcezza mia*, I am freezing to death," he growled at her.

But she didn't move. She only peered up at him, looking about as happy to see him as he had been to find her gone. It did nothing to soothe his frayed temper.

Just as it made something in him turn over to find her looking so effortlessly lovely, here in this lonely cottage so far away from the world. So far away from *him*.

He did not often see her this way. Unstyled and wholly natural. Tiziano had woken up with her these many mornings, it was true, but there were always more pressing things to do with her. Then there were calls to take and engagements to avoid, and by the time he saw her again in the evenings, her attendants had always had their way with her. And they had proved remarkably talented at creating the vision he'd had of her from the start.

But it was this Annie who made his chest hurt.

Her red-gold hair was piled on the top of her head, but not in some elegant chignon. It was a mess of curls, pinned haphazardly to sit slightly off-center at the top of her head. Her eyes were big and gray, and rimmed with red. And all he could really focus on was that spray of freckles like stardust over her nose and the way she pulled her lower lip between her teeth that would now and forever remind him of the night she'd given him her innocence.

And she had *taken* all of this from him.

"Annie," he said, and there was an urgency in his own voice he barely understood. "Let me in."

For a moment that stretched on far too long, she appeared to consider it.

And for the very first time, possibly ever, Tiziano Accardi had to confront the possibility that a woman might, in fact, slam a door in his face.

More, she might mean it.

But instead, Annie blew out a breath. Then she stepped back and waved a hand, as if she was *surrendering* to his presence.

Tiziano wanted nothing so much as to stalk inside in a manner clearly showing his displeasure, but the house was tiny and ridiculous. More suitable for a mouse than a man. He was forced to stoop down, then pretzel himself inside, following her down a haphazard hallway to what passed for a sitting room.

He could see in an instant that this was likely the only room that Annie had ventured into since her arrival, which could only have been a few hours ago. Some of the furniture was still covered. There were Christmas carols playing on an ancient wireless. She'd made a kind of nest for herself on a faded-looking sofa, piled high with quilts. And there was a fire in the grate, crackling merrily away and throwing about the only light.

She went and sat on that couch, looking prim and proper, but she was dressed in clothes he didn't recognize. Because he hadn't seen her in anything but gowns or workwear. Ever. And it was astonishing to him that the simple sight of a woman in an offhandedly elegant cashmere sweater thrown so carelessly over an old pair of jeans should make his heart flip around in his chest. Quite like it was trying to escape.

"Tell me, Annie," he said, hearing too much darkness in his voice but doing nothing to stop it. "Why is it you have come to this abandoned house in the middle of nowhere, to sit by a lonely fire, without bothering to leave so much as a note?"

She studied him. And he, who normally adored being stared at, found that today, it made him… Not uncomfortable. Not exactly.

But it was harder to remain still than it should have been.

"It's Christmas," she said.

"I'm well aware." Though he could not say that without a pang of guilt, thinking of Catriona and her family. Not to mention the staff in Hampstead, who he had gruffly ordered to take the rest of the year off.

"It's Christmas, Tiziano, and I spoke with Victoria Cameron myself last night." Annie's gray gaze was solemn, but this time, he found it far less steadying. "She has no intention of marrying you. So you see, our arrangement is already at its end. I saw no need to draw it out."

He stared at her. "You saw...?" He shook his head, as if that could keep him from feeling as if his ribs were tearing him open from the inside out. *"You saw no need?"*

And though she was dressed more like the secretary he'd met in that stairwell than the pampered lover he'd made her since, the way she folded her hands in her lap and smiled at him was 100 percent the fantasy mistress he'd created for his own purposes these last weeks. Her expression was serene. Her smile bordered on lazy.

There was even a hint of something like pity in her gaze.

Meaning, none of it was Annie.

But she was speaking. "I fulfilled all my contractual obligations to you. You're welcome to check."

"I do not make it a habit of wandering about with contracts in my back pocket. Odd, I know."

Annie only looked calmer. "This was always to be

our end date. I think you know that. Just as I think your objection has nothing to do with me personally. Or anything that passed between us. It's simply that you're used to being in control of these kinds of things." She inclined her head. "And I apologize. I should have given you the option to end this yourself this morning, as we both know you would have."

Tiziano knew no such thing. It hadn't even crossed his mind to end things with her today.

And the ramifications of that hit him, then.

Hard enough that if he hadn't already been standing near a wall, he might've stumbled back to find one, the better to prop himself up while a different sort of storm swept him away.

And all the while, Annie was watching him closely. Looking something like vindicated, as if she'd expected precisely this response.

But she couldn't possibly have done. Because he hadn't been planning to end things with her this morning.

He hadn't been planning to end things with her at all.

Last night, when they'd left the Christmas Eve ball with no hint of the threatened engagement, the Tiziano he'd been when this had all started would have ended things in the car. He would have dropped her at the hotel of her choice and would have had Catriona pop by in the next day or two to help sort out where she intended to go next. He would have washed his hands of her and forgotten her by morning, when he would have jetted off somewhere warm to reacquaint himself with his love of the bikini.

Because the game had been successful. The show had done what it was meant to do. And Tiziano had always known exactly when to draw the curtain.

Instead, he'd taken Annie home. Because that crypt of a house was as much a home as anywhere else. He had taken her to her bedroom, to be more precise, because he would have gone anywhere she was.

It hadn't even crossed his mind to finish with her.

And it still hadn't.

Clearly.

For here he was. Standing in a house he barely fit into. It was as if he'd crawled into one of those gingerbread houses that had never featured much in his Italian childhood. He might as well have inserted himself among the gumdrops, and why?

Because she was here.

Against his will and despite his best intentions, Annie Meeks had not simply threatened his languid unconcern—the hallmark of his identity, he would have said.

She'd upended everything.

And Tiziano had been so busy telling himself that he was playing a part that he'd completely missed the fact that he'd stopped *playing* a long time ago.

He hadn't been *pretending* to fall in love. He hadn't been *acting* as if he'd lost the plot completely over an inappropriate secretary who his brother would consider excluded from consideration by virtue of the simple fact she'd agreed to this game in the first place. Not even getting into her social status or the fact she'd been a secretary in their company.

Tiziano hadn't been *putting on an act* at all. He hadn't been faking a thing.

He'd shown Annie more of himself than he'd ever shown anyone, save his own mirror.

And she'd left him anyway.

Something rolled through him, a dark kind of anguish, but he told himself it was outrage.

"It turned out we were both a bit better at this than we expected," Annie was saying, still watching him in that way he didn't like. But then, he didn't like any of this. "But it's time we retreat to our separate corners and finish the way we always planned. To be honest, I'm ready for it to be over." She lifted her chin, possibly in response to whatever expression was on his face. For once, Tiziano had no idea. "The holiday season is all but over. This level of intensity won't be necessary going forward, even if the threat of engagement was still hanging over you. It's better this way."

He let out a laugh then and it must have sounded as unbalanced as he felt, because her eyes went wide.

"But I do not agree," he said, his voice low. That current of anguish wrapping tight around him, until it became him. "Perhaps you have forgotten, Annie, that I have had a great many lovers in my time. You have had only the one."

And he could admit it was a pleasure to see an emotion he hadn't seen a hint of so far move over her face then. Her cheeks lit up, red with temper, and he liked it.

He reveled in it, in fact.

"I don't need a reminder of your favorite pastime, Tiziano." Her eyes shot fire at him. "I can't wait to live it with you through the pages of all your favorite tabloids as you take it up again."

Once upon a time, some six weeks ago, Tiziano would have told anyone within earshot that jealousy was the province of the childish, the unfashionably *intense.*

Now he felt it was, truly, the very least of the things she should feel at the prospect of him with other women.

Given that the notion of her with any other man, ever, made him feel as close to murderous as he had ever been.

Still, he was not so far gone that he did not recall that the woman he'd met in that stairwell—the woman who had been completely unimpressed with him in every respect—would not have cared in the least what he did or who he did it with.

That blaze of red on her cheeks wasn't only temper.

To him, it was hope.

"I think you are in love with me, Annie." His voice was quiet, but he aimed every word with deadly accuracy. "I think that you raced away in the night, on Christmas morning, no less, because you know you've broken the rules."

He watched her pull in a breath, as if to steady herself. He watched a kind of misery move through her eyes, and he hated it.

But the hands in her lap curled into fists. "You bought my performance, Tiziano." Her voice was cold. "And my performance is what you got. You have no right to my feelings, and thank goodness. Because you're wrong."

He might have accepted that, or tried, but he heard that little hitch in her voice.

"I don't believe you, *dolcezza*," he murmured.

And as he watched, as he *hoped*, something rolled through Annie. He could see her go pale, then flush bright again—before she dissolved into tears.

She pushed to her feet, so that they were now facing off in this tiny little room, surrounded on all sides by the ghosts of a long life, shrouded in old sheets and surrounded by dusty pictures.

It felt entirely too much like his childhood for his liking.

But even as he thought that, he knew that everything had changed. It wasn't only that he was older. Hopefully wiser, if only by default. But that he recognized himself now, the way he never had before.

And Tiziano had no intention of being a dusty portrait on this wall or any other one.

"You got everything you wanted," Annie threw at him, her voice thick and those tears wetting her cheeks. "And it's all been a rousing success. I haven't broken any rules. No one works on Christmas anyway. Even if we have to make another appearance, it won't be today. There is no reason at all for you to be here."

It was as if he'd never seen her before. Because he'd been so busy pretending, hadn't he, that he didn't see what was so plainly in front of him now.

But now he did. It seemed to him, suddenly, that he always had.

"Try again," he suggested.

She vibrated a little, there where she stood with her cute little feet in thick, patterned socks. That glorious scowl of hers taking over her face. As if, he thought then—understanding dawning—as if she was fighting the urge to cry.

"Tiziano," she said, and her voice was different now. Lower. Rougher. "I know who you are. And I know what you want. I've watched you all these weeks, in your element. You like a show." Her voice cracked on that, and so his heart did, too. "There's nothing wrong with that. But the show can only go on for so long. Sooner or later, reality reasserts itself."

He started to say something, but Annie shook her head, looking even fiercer. "Not for you. I understand that. But for *me*. And I…" The breath she sucked in sounded ragged. "I can't go on pretending to be madly in love with you every night. I can't carry on acting the part of your besotted mistress. I can't do it."

"Because it isn't true?" he asked, with a kind of soft menace. "Or because it is?"

And he thought she would throw something at him. Call out another storm, put her temper to work. But instead, she seemed to deflate before him, and he liked that far less.

She hugged herself, but this was Annie, so she kept that steady gray gaze on him all the while.

"You're right," she said, as if it cost her dearly to say it out loud. "I love you."

Something in him roared, deep and long.

Yet she wasn't finished. "But I love *you*, Tiziano. And I know who you are. Please do me the favor of recognizing who I am, too. You told me it would be two weeks. It's been six. I can't do it anymore. I'm not cut out for acting. I can't pretend."

"No, *dolcezza mia*," he agreed. "You're a terrible actor." He laughed a little when she scowled at him again. "But don't you see? When it comes to boring parties where someone is called upon to be entertaining, I have never encountered a spotlight I could not hog. When it comes to tedious dinner parties where there must always be a clown, who better to assume that role than one such as I, who has never taken himself seriously? But when it comes to love, *amore mio*, I have never managed to convince anyone that I've even heard of such a thing."

She shook her head at that as if she didn't understand him. "Then we're in agreement. It's over.

No more performances. No more pretending. No more—"

"Annie, *dolcezza mia, amore mio*, I have been acting all my life," he said, cutting her off. "The bad influence, the disappointment—I played down to the lowest expectations of me wherever I went. When I was sent away to school, I was the Italian clown, because it was easier to make them laugh than sit in my own loneliness." He had never said that out loud before, but this was Annie. He could tell her anything. "I have never met a moment I couldn't make a stage, and there has never been a bit of scenery available that I couldn't chew. Because the best way to disappear in plain sight is to make the whole world think that you're nothing but a shallow puddle."

"That is not who you are," she threw at him, fiercely.

"No," he agreed, his gaze intent on hers. "But you are the only one who took one look at this disguise that has fooled countless people in all walks of life and saw straight through to the real me. The only one. Ever."

"Tiziano…" she whispered.

"This has never been acting," he told her, from that place where his chest hurt the most. "I think I loved you from the first moment I saw you, laid low before me, yet uncowed. Undiminished. Completely yourself from the very first. It was impossible to be near you and not wish to do the same. To be completely me, however I could."

Her eyes were too bright. "You don't mean that."

"I have never meant anything more."

He moved to her then, because he could no longer keep himself away. Then he took her in his arms, knowing in the moment her hands came to rest on his chest that he could breathe again.

For the first time since he'd woken up to find her gone, he could breathe.

"I don't want a mistress, Annie," he told her, as if the words came from him of their own accord. Called out from the deepest part of him, all for her. "I want *you*. I want every part of you. I don't want to hide any longer. I don't want all of these parties and all of these pointless people, not when I have you. Because everyone looks at me, Annie. I imagine they always will. But you alone see me."

"Since the very first moment," she whispered, her fingers gripping him as if she needed to hold on as hard as he did. "It's as if I've never truly seen anything else."

"You must decide if you are ready for this," he warned her. "Because I intend to be demanding." And he shook his head at the expression on her face then. "Not only in bed. I want every part of you. I want to marry you and grow old with you. All of these things that never made sense to me before, I want to build with you. I want babies who we can raise, you and I, to be more than heirs and spares, shunted off into roles we pick for them before their births. I want them to be so loved, so adored, that it would never occur to them to spend a lifetime pretending to be things they are not."

"Oh, Tiziano," she breathed, and the tears flowed openly down her cheeks now. "I think I must be dreaming."

His heart was beating hard again. This time, he liked it. "Then I'm dreaming with you."

"I love you," she told him, tipping her head back so he could see that she meant it, all over her lovely face. It blazed there in her gray eyes, as sure as steel. "And I thought that loving you meant leaving you, because I don't want you to feel badly that you can't give me the things I want from you when you don't even know what they are. Because how could you know? But then, everyone I love has died, or betrayed me, so it's not as if I'm any expert, am I?"

"I will never betray you," he promised her, and something lit up within him when he said it. As if he had branded himself with that vow, deep inside. "Everything I know of love, I have learned from you, Annie. I promise you, no matter what happens, that love will come first. We will make it so."

"I don't think life works like that," she whispered, though her eyes were gleaming.

And he smiled then, running his thumbs over her cheeks to capture the excess moisture there, and wiping it away.

"I am Tiziano Accardi," he told her. "Life works precisely as I wish it to work." He waited for her to smile, and then he bent his head to hers. "Come, *dolcezza mia*. Let me show you."

And he did.

CHAPTER TWELVE

THE SNOW KEPT COMING, but Annie didn't care. Because inside her grandmother's spellbound little cottage, she had a fire. Better still, she had her love.

It was, by far, the most magical Christmas ever.

When the weather cleared on Boxing Day, they ventured out, but only to gather enough supplies at the small local market that they could come back and hunker down some more.

But Tiziano was Tiziano, after all, so by the time they returned there was a Christmas tree, decorated with all the trimmings, standing near the fireplace as if it had always been there.

Annie thought that her nan would have been pleased.

Then she and the billionaire who had made her his mistress sat on the floor near the fire and ate beans on toast, which Tiziano found vile no matter how many times Annie assured him it was a true British delicacy.

And as the years rolled by, they regarded that

funny little Christmas as their true wedding and the two weeks they spent in her grandmother's cottage their real honeymoon.

They had a proper wedding two years later.

Tiziano insisted that it be a proper paparazzi-friendly affair, complete with a church ceremony and a star-studded reception, because the most notorious mistress of the modern era deserved her happy ending.

Printed in all the same papers that had spent so much time speculating about her.

"No one cares about the fact I was your mistress," she told him the night before the ceremony. Tiziano flatly refused to spend the night, or any night, apart—no matter how traditional it was meant to be. "No one cares about us, either. The only time they ever will again will be when we break up."

He pulled her to him, there in the bright and cheerful kitchen of the only property they lived in these days. It was a property they had found and moved into together. Then made a home together. Unlike his other London properties, now rented out, this one was filled with warmth. Light. *Them*. Annie had made the attic her studio and had found her way back to painting—after finishing her degree course at Goldsmith's.

She had even dared to have her first show, which the papers had all begrudgingly admitted was not bad. For a novice.

Tiziano, in the meantime, had stopped pretending he didn't know how to get to Accardi Industries headquarters.

Together, they had figured out not only how to love each other, but how to follow their dreams. No hiding required.

Here in his arms in the home they'd made, Annie smiled up at this man, the love of her life. She could have told him that they would begin raising their family here sooner than planned, but she didn't. Because she wanted to enjoy his reaction without having to worry about entertaining half of Europe the next day, as it was certain to be epic.

"It is a shame, then," Tiziano said, smiling down at her, his blue eyes warm and bright and hers. All hers. "We must resign ourselves to the obscurity you once longed for, *dolcezza*. For we will never break up. Not as long as we both live."

And to the great disappointment of the phalanxes of women who remained hopeful they might yet get the chance with him, they never did.

Though there were a lot of tears at the wedding, all the same.

Roxy, back from Australia and charmed, despite herself, by her sister's solid relationship, walked her down the aisle.

"I should steal your credit card more often," she said as they made their way toward the altar, where Tiziano stood like a dream come true, dressed entirely in handcrafted Italian glory and Annie's favorite smile. The one that was all for her.

Annie slid a look at her sister. "Don't push your luck."

But they were both laughing. And later that year, they went, just the two of them, to the holiday park they'd visited as kids. They sat by the sea on typically frigid British summer days. They danced to old songs on the radio, and burnt their sausages in the pan. And then, afterward, went and got their feet in the dirt in Nan's garden.

After the ceremony was done and Tiziano kissed her far longer than necessary in the church, Annie danced with his best man. And despite the occasion, Ago was no less stern than she remembered him from long ago.

"You once told me that your brother's duty would never be me," she reminded him.

But Ago had been changed by these years, too, and he laughed. "Never," he agreed. "Thank goodness." His stern gaze found hers, and lightened. "It appears what you are instead is his heart, and I think he'd be the first to agree that he's a better man for it."

Annie's smile trembled a little on her mouth, then. "I hope so."

And as the years passed, there were hardships. There were tears. There was no one season to life. For all the flowers that spring brought to bloom, there was always the coming fall.

But what she remembered most were the summers. The endless sunshine and the sweetest, softest days.

So bright they seemed to make the harder, colder seasons fade away.

And a few times a year, she and Tiziano stole away from their lives, and their gray-eyed, dangerously charming children. They holed up together in that little cottage in the Cotswolds. If it was winter, they sat by the fire and told each other stories of their brighter days—some already past and some yet ahead. In the spring, they wandered the garden, where Annie taught her aristocratic husband to plant seeds. How to put his hands in the earth. How to plant hope into dirt and wait for the rain to make it into flowers.

In the summer they would dance beneath the stars, the garden dizzy with flowers and vines. And in the fall, they would walk hand in hand in the cool mornings, the nostalgia all around them like mist. Yet laced straight through with joy.

And then, without fail, they would steal away to their favorite bed beneath the eaves and learn each other all over again.

Again and again, as if they were new.

* * * * *

#4065 THE ITALIAN'S BRIDE WORTH BILLIONS
by Lynne Graham

Gianni *must* restore his reputation when the rumor mill threatens his position as CEO. Asking childhood friend Josephine to be his convenient bride is his first task...and pretending their married life doesn't feel deliciously real is his second!

#4066 THE ACCIDENTAL ACCARDI HEIR
The Outrageous Accardi Brothers
by Caitlin Crews

Proud, dutiful Ago is quick to make amends to his brother's jilted bride, Victoria. But he intended only to apologize, *not* to take the beautiful heiress to bed! Now, months later, the Italian hears Victoria's shocking news... She's having his child!

#4067 RULES OF THEIR ROYAL WEDDING NIGHT
Scandalous Royal Weddings
by Michelle Smart

After marrying solely for convenience and to produce an heir, Crown Prince Amadeo doesn't expect to find such passion on his wedding night. He senses there's more to shy Elsbeth than she reveals, but duty-bound Amadeo cannot allow emotion to distract him...can he?

#4068 HIS PREGNANT DESERT QUEEN
Brothers of the Desert
by Maya Blake

Playboy and spare heir Prince Javid never dreamed of ruling, and he certainly never imagined needing a convenient marriage to lady-in-waiting Anaïs to take his crown! Only, their honeymoon sparks much more than their arrangement promised...*including* a shocking consequence!

HPCNMRA1122

#4069 A BABY SCANDAL IN ITALY
by Chantelle Shaw

Penniless Ivy is shocked to discover she's exposed the wrong man as her orphaned nephew's father! Now, to stop the truth from ripping Rafael's life apart, Ivy must wear his ring...and bind them all together!

#4070 THE COST OF CINDERELLA'S CONFESSION
by Julia James

To free her cousin from an unwanted marriage, Ariana must confess—one night with the groom, Luca, left her pregnant! She knows the lie will incur the billionaire's wrath. But going toe-to-toe with vengeful Luca is a wild and unexpectedly passionate ride!

#4071 STRANDED WITH MY FORBIDDEN BILLIONAIRE
by Lucy King

When I won millions in the lottery, I knew superrich financier Nick was the only person I could rely on to help me. But when a tropical storm on his island has us stuck together—indefinitely—how long can we control our dangerously growing attraction?

#4072 THE WIFE THE SPANIARD NEVER FORGOT
by Pippa Roscoe

An amnesia misdiagnosis provides the ideal opportunity for Javier to finally discover why his estranged wife, Emily, left. And to remind her of the connection he's not ready to forget...not when every heated look makes it clear she still feels it, too!

Get 4 FREE REWARDS!

We'll send you 2 FREE Books plus 2 FREE Mystery Gifts.

FREE
Value Over
$20

Both the **Harlequin® Desire** and **Harlequin Presents®** series feature compelling novels filled with passion, sensuality and intriguing scandals.

YES! Please send me 2 FREE novels from the Harlequin Desire or Harlequin Presents series and my 2 FREE gifts (gifts are worth about $10 retail). After receiving them, if I don't wish to receive any more books, I can return the shipping statement marked "cancel." If I don't cancel, I will receive 6 brand-new Harlequin Presents Larger-Print books every month and be billed just $6.05 each in the U.S. or $6.24 each in Canada, a savings of at least 10% off the cover price or 6 Harlequin Desire books every month and be billed just $4.80 each in the U.S. or $5.49 each in Canada, a savings of at least 13% off the cover price. It's quite a bargain! Shipping and handling is just 50¢ per book in the U.S. and $1.25 per book in Canada.* I understand that accepting the 2 free books and gifts places me under no obligation to buy anything. I can always return a shipment and cancel at any time by calling the number below. The free books and gifts are mine to keep no matter what I decide.

Choose one: ☐ **Harlequin Desire**   ☐ **Harlequin Presents Larger-Print**
                    (225/326 HDN GRTW)   (176/376 HDN GQ9Z)

Name (please print)

Address   Apt. #

City   State/Province   Zip/Postal Code

Email: Please check this box ☐ if you would like to receive newsletters and promotional emails from Harlequin Enterprises ULC and its affiliates. You can unsubscribe anytime.

Mail to the Harlequin Reader Service:
IN U.S.A.: P.O. Box 1341, Buffalo, NY 14240-8531
IN CANADA: P.O. Box 603, Fort Erie, Ontario L2A 5X3

Want to try 2 free books from another series? Call 1-800-873-8635 or visit www.ReaderService.com.
